THE CURSE OF
CROOKED ELBOW

AN ARMITAGE HUMP MYSTERY

DAVID CODD

1.'CHICKEN.'

Benjamin Bottomley-Belch was the editor of The Passing Print school newspaper.

I didn't like him. Not in the slightest. But then not many people did. And yet, funnily enough, nobody ever dared to tell him. Not to his face, anyway. Come to think of it, nobody ever dared to argue with him at all.

Until now …

'It's not fair!' I cried, slamming my hand down on the table. I regretted it a moment later when the pain shot up and down my wrist. 'Why do I always get the worst possible jobs to report on?' I grumbled through gritted teeth. 'Tell me? I want to know.'

Benjamin – also known as Benny the Bottom – stopped pacing the room and straightened his tie. He was a small, round boy with flushed cheeks and a seemingly permanent smirk that, if dreams came true, I would've loved to have wiped from his face.

'I don't know what you mean,' he replied, grinning from ear to ear.

'Yes, you do,' I snapped back at him. 'In the past month I've reported on stinking sewers … leaking lavatories … the dangers of dog poo and the state of sick-splattered side-streets!'

Benny rolled his eyes at me. 'Have you finished yet, Miss Coddle? Rant over?'

I hated it when he did that. Used my surname. Why didn't he just call me Molly like any normal thirteen-year-old? Yes, that's right. Molly Coddle. Hilarious, isn't it? No, really. I'm rolling about on the floor here. I can barely breathe it's so amusing.

The dictionary definition of mollycoddle is to treat someone in an indulgent or overprotective way.

Benny, however, treated me like something you'd find hanging from a monkey's armpit.

'No, I haven't finished yet,' I said firmly. 'Not by a long shot.'

'Oh, I think you have,' remarked Benny, dismissing me with a wave of his hand. 'Have you heard yourself recently? Your voice … it's like a swarm of bees at an over-crowded singing contest. Just a horrible buzzing sound that refuses to fade away.'

I clenched my fists under the table. The way I saw it there were two ways this could go. I could either jump up and whack Benny on the end of his piggy nose, or I could start to cry.

I knew which one I preferred, but I also knew which one was most likely to happen.

'Look at me, look at me,' whined Benny, flapping his arms about like an excitable penguin. 'I get all the worst jobs … I don't deserve this … boo-hoo. Ha! You've really embarrassed yourself this time, Miss Coddle. It gives me no pleasure to do this, but maybe it's about time I spelt it out for you.'

'Yes, why don't you?' I said snottily. 'Spell it out for all of us.'

I peered around the newsroom (also known as the school canteen) for support, but none was forthcoming. Aside from me and Benny, there were four other children in attendance at the daily meeting of The Passing Print. Two boys and two girls. And, as far as I was aware, not one of them had ever been asked to report on anything as revolting as missing manure at McMulch's farm.

Benny puffed out his chest. 'With great power comes great responsibility,' he began pompously. 'The Passing Print is my life. It means more to me than both my mother and father put together. I'd rather cut off every single toe on my left foot than see this newspaper fold.'

'Tell me if you need any help with that,' I muttered under my breath.

'Tough decisions don't scare me,' continued Benny, sweeping his floppy fringe to one side. 'I'm not here to make friends, Miss Coddle – I'm here to make the greatest school newspaper that the town of Passing Wind has ever known!'

One of the girls jumped up and started to clap. Her name was Ursula Fawn, but that wasn't the most irritating thing about her.

'Benjamin is here to make the greatest school newspaper that the town of Passing Wind has ever known,' she repeated word for word.

Yes, *that* was the most irritating thing about her.

'Good for Benjamin,' I mumbled. 'What I still don't understand, however, is why I get all the worst stories to report on?'

'There is a pecking order,' explained Benny. 'From top to bottom. From great to … erm … not so great. I, naturally, am at the peak of the mountain. If there's something important going on then I'm always there. I'm talking robberies … explosions … murders—'

'Murders?' I couldn't believe my ears. 'The closest we've ever come to a murder in Passing Wind is when Mrs Smoulder accidentally set fire to her husband when he was cleaning the chimney.'

'Yes … and who was there to report on it?' said Benny, pointing at himself. 'After me, we have Miss Fawn. She's a regular contributor to the newspaper, not to mention my biggest supporter. Then there's the Slumber brothers, Marty and Barty. They tend to work together on the less … challenging stories, whilst our fifth member, Miss Chip, will often … *chip* in whenever the chance arises. Admittedly, what the other four offer isn't exactly headline grabbing, but look long and hard enough and I'm sure you'll find something from each and every one of them somewhere within our publication. Page thirty-three perhaps—'

'There are only thirty-two pages in the entire newspaper,' I remarked.

'Oh, my mistake,' chuckled Benny. 'So, just to be clear, Miss Coddle, the pecking order begins with my good self … then it moves onto my four other friends … and finally, both last and regrettably least, it ends with—'

'Me,' I said, beating him to it.

'Yes, you,' nodded Benny. 'Everybody has to start at the bottom—'

'You didn't,' I argued.

'It's my newspaper,' replied Benny.

'It's Benjamin's newspaper,' repeated Ursula.

'What I say goes,' Benny insisted. 'I'm the boss. The king of the castle.'

'Benjamin's the king of the castle,' echoed Ursula. 'And I'm his queen.'

Benny turned his nose up in disgust. 'We're not that close, Miss Fawn. Just work colleagues. Right, if that's all you have to say, Miss Coddle, then I think we'll move on. Time is precious in the fast-paced world of news reporting. These are valuable minutes we're wasting talking about you and your … personal problems.'

I was at boiling point. Given half a chance, there was nothing I wanted more than to storm out of the newsroom.

I wanted to … but knew I couldn't.

More than anything, I loved to write, and The Passing Print was the only publication in town where I would get the opportunity (however small that opportunity may be).

'Your silence speaks volumes,' said Benny, spinning away from me. 'Right, where were we? Ah, Armitage Hump. Are any of you any closer to securing an interview with him?'

'Yes, are any of you any closer to securing an interview with him?' said Ursula, before answering her own question. 'No, I'm not, Benjamin. Sorry, Benjamin. I'll try not to let you down again, Benjamin.'

'Anybody else?' asked a clearly irritated Benny.

One of the boys peeled his face off the table and began to rub his eyes. I guessed it was Marty, but I couldn't be certain. 'Armitage who?' he yawned.

'Hump!' screamed Benny. 'Armitage Hump! The famous private detective. Did you or your brother get to meet him?'

Marty took a moment to think. And then another moment after that because thinking clearly didn't come easily to him. 'Nope,' he mumbled eventually. 'We did hear him, though. He spoke to us when we rang his doorbell. Just the two words—'

'Let me guess,' frowned Benny. 'He told you to get lost.'

'No, nothing like that,' said Marty. 'He told us to go away.'

'That's the same thing,' sighed Benny.

'Is it?' Marty seemed surprised. 'That Hump fella said it really loud as well. And not just once either. Twenty-three times in total. He only stopped when we did as he asked. We went away.'

A frustrated Benny began to pace the floor. 'Well, that's that then,' he muttered. 'You've all tried and you've all failed. It would seem that Armitage Hump is not a man to be—'

'I'll do it,' I said suddenly. Unfortunately, I didn't stop there. 'I'll get an interview with Armitage Hump. It'll be a front page story.'

'You?' Benny leant over the table and pressed a finger against my forehead. 'You?'

'Yes, me,' I said, swatting his hand away. 'I can do it. I know I can.'

The newsroom fell silent for six long seconds … before Benny started to laugh on the seventh. 'Didn't you hear me, Miss Coddle? They've all tried—'

'*They've* all tried – *I* haven't,' I argued.

'And there's a reason for that,' continued Benny. 'Armitage Hump may be a famous private detective, but he's also the rudest, grumpiest, most foul-tempered man in the whole of Passing Wind. He doesn't like talking to people. No, that's not true. He doesn't like people full stop! So, with that in mind, why would he possibly want to give an interview to you? You're a nobody, Miss Coddle. A complete non-entity. No, I really don't think there's any point—'

'Are you scared?' I asked.

Benny stopped and stared at me. 'Scared?'

'Scared that I'll succeed where the rest of you have failed,' I said.

'I'm not scared of anything,' replied Benny. 'Especially not you. And, for your information, I never fail. That's a fact. And if it looks as if I might then Father always comes to my rescue.' Benny threw up his hands. 'Okay, have it your way, Miss Coddle. I accept your challenge.'

'Challenge?' Now it was my turn to look confused. 'What challenge?'

'Oh, don't tell me you're backing out already,' said Benny, shaking his head at me. 'Not only are you a rubbish reporter, you're also a chicken.'

'I am neither a rubbish reporter nor a chicken,' I said

firmly. 'I just don't know what you're talking about. Who said anything about a challenge?'

'You did, Miss Coddle,' insisted Benny. 'If you manage to get an interview with Armitage Hump, then I'll give you the front page. Not only that, but you'll have proved yourself. You can have better reporting jobs after that. If you fail, however …' The smile on Benny's toad-like face began to widen. 'Then you're out,' he remarked.

It took a moment for that to sink in. 'Out?'

'Your days writing for The Passing Print will be over,' Benny explained. 'I never want to see you anywhere near this newsroom again. That's the challenge, Miss Coddle. You can either take it or leave it.'

Oh, this was tricky. My heart said *yes*, but my head said *no*. The rest of my body, meanwhile, just wanted to get out of there as quickly as possible. Yes, I was desperate to write, but what I didn't want, however, was to spend another minute in the company of my odious editor.

'Cluck-cluck,' said Benny, flapping his arms about. 'Just as I expected. All mouth and nothing to back it up.'

I could feel myself beginning to blush as, one by one, the others started to giggle.

'Challenge accepted,' I blurted out. 'I'll get that interview … just you see.'

The breath caught in my throat as I stood up and rushed towards the door. I had to get out of there.

'One last thing, Miss Coddle,' called out Benny. I stopped, but refused to turn. 'Take a good look around because, unless I'm mistaken, this'll be the last time you ever set foot in this newsroom,' he said. 'You know the rules. No interview, no coming back. I would thank you for your contribution, but then you haven't really done much, have you?'

My entire body was shaking as I left the newsroom and hurried along the corridor.

What had I done?

No, really.

What … had … I … done?

2.'BOOK.'

To my surprise, it wasn't that difficult to track down Armitage Hump.

Not if you asked the right people. And since everybody I asked seemed to know exactly where he lived then I suppose that makes everybody I asked the right person.

Babbling Brook, however, was particularly helpful. Both the local librarian and a world-class gossip, I went to see her straight after school. It took less than three minutes to find out exactly what I needed to know ... and then another sixteen to get away from her! Those sixteen minutes, though, were a small price to pay for the information she provided.

This is the shortened version of what she told me.

'Armitage Hump? Oh, he's a rum 'un, make no mistake. Keeps himself to himself, so he does. Not overly fond of folk pestering him. Where's he live? Tipsy Towers, the last I heard. It's a whopping great three-storey house on the outskirts of Passing Wind. That's if you can call it a house – I'd call it one big gust away from a pile of bricks! Our Mr Hump lives alone on the ground floor. Look a little higher and you'll find Professor Cracker-Boom at the top of the

Towers. He's as mad as a box of beavers, but completely harmless. Morning and Evelyn Darling are right in the middle, squashed between a Hump and a Cracker-Boom. That's an unfortunate sandwich for anyone to stomach! They're nice though, the Darlings. Very musical. Lots of dancing. Mrs Goose, the landlady, lurks down in the basement … and that's exactly where she belongs! Heed my words, young Molly, the Goose is best avoided at all costs!'

I stored that information somewhere safe (in my head, not my pocket) and headed for home.

Tomorrow was Saturday.

And Saturday was the day I would go and see Armitage Hump.

Seventeen hours later I was stood on the doorstep of Tipsy Towers.

It was hardly the most desirable dwelling in Passing Wind, but I had seen worse. Probably. I tried to rack my brains, but couldn't quite recall even one other house that leant so unnaturally to one side. If anything, it reminded me of a three-legged cow in a hurricane. Having said that, how many three-legged cows have you seen with filth-encrusted windows, crumbling brickwork and a lopsided roof that was missing more than half its tiles?

If I was stood on the doorstep then there had to be a door in front of me. This one had been crudely painted in yellow, although that same paint had long since started to crack and peel. To the left of the door there was a battered, old intercom system. I rested my finger on the button for

Armitage Hump, but then hesitated whilst I took a breath. Then I took another. And another. And another after that.

Whether I liked it or not, I knew I had to press it eventually.

'Here goes nothing.' I prodded the button and then quickly removed my finger as the intercom crackled and fizzed.

Almost immediately, a man's voice growled out of the speaker. 'Go away!'

With that, the crackling – much like our conversation – came to an abrupt halt.

I lifted my hand for a second time, but then left it dangling in mid-air. What was I scared of? I was still trying to figure that out when my finger seemed to move by itself and jabbed at the button. Once again, the intercom crackled into life before the same voice answered.

'Seriously?' he muttered. 'Twice in ten seconds? Oh, why don't you just come on in and be done with it!'

I screwed up my face. 'Really?'

'No, of course not really, you witless wombat,' the voice snapped. 'Why would I possibly want to let you into my apartment? You could be anything. A man … a woman … a child. Yuck! I dislike children immensely. They're unnaturally small and horrendously smelly. And sneaky. Ever so sneaky. Not to be trusted in the slightest.' The voice paused. 'You're not a child, are you?'

'I'm a newspaper reporter,' I replied. 'I write for The Passing Print—'

'Let me stop you there,' said the voice, doing just that by

interrupting me. 'I dislike newspaper reporters even more than children. And as for a combination of the two ... I think I'm going to go now before I throw up all over my trousers!'

'Wait!' I said hastily.

'Not possible,' insisted the voice. 'Can't you see I've got my hands full?'

'No, obviously not,' I said, staring at the intercom. 'I can't *see* you at all. Talking of which, don't you know it's rude to leave someone waiting on your doorstep?'

'Rude?' There was a curious snorting sound, like a laugh gone horribly wrong. 'That's marvellous,' the voice remarked. 'I love being rude. And on this occasion I wasn't even trying. Ah, that's cheered me up no end. Hold on ... no, it hasn't. I'm still as miserable as ever. Right, you can go away now ... get lost ... goodbye and good riddance!'

I had to do something and fast.

'I'm ... writing a book,' I spluttered. The man fell silent. I just hoped he couldn't tell that I was making it up on the spot. 'A book about all of your cases,' I continued. 'You are the great Armitage Hump, after all. The famous private detective—'

'Wrong!' argued the man. 'I'm not a famous private detective – I'm a private famous detective. There's a big difference. Get it right next time.'

'So, you are Armitage Hump then?' I said, grinning to myself.

The man groaned. 'Of course I am ... careful! Watch where you're putting that thing!'

'Are you okay?' I asked, edging closer to the speaker. 'What just happened?'

'What just happened is I nearly got my head chopped off!' yelled the man I now knew to be Armitage Hump.

A moment later the intercom cut off, but this time it was followed by a loud *click*. I pushed down on the handle, surprised to find that the door was open. Without pausing for thought, I slipped inside.

There was no turning back now.

The door closed behind me and I found myself in a dark, dismal hallway that smelled remarkably similar to a compost heap on a rainy day. The walls were grey whilst the carpet was brown (although that's not to say that brown was its original colour). There was a staircase to my right that led all the way up to the other apartments. Closer than that, however, there was a light switch. I pressed it, but nothing happened. Frustrated, I pressed it several more times before shifting my gaze to the ceiling. The light fitting may have been covered in a lifetime's worth of dust, but I could still see that it was missing a bulb.

'Mr Hump,' I shouted, but there was no reply. Using the wall to guide me, I started to make my way cautiously through the gloom, my target a door at the end of the hallway. I quickly removed my hands, however, when huge chunks of plaster crumbled beneath my fingertips.

'Mr Hump,' I called out for a second time. I could hear noises in the distance. Grunts and groans and the occasional yelp. They were coming from behind the door.

I was almost within touching distance when some kind

of foul-smelling creature crept out of the shadows. I tried to scream, but it caught in my throat. I was still trying when I realised it wasn't a creature at all, but something else entirely.

A woman.

I think. It was hard to tell. Quite simply, her face was the stuff of nightmares. My only guess was that it had been squashed and squeezed in every possible direction by a rusty mangle, before being beaten to a pulp with a king-size rolling pin. Every hour. Of every day. For the past twenty years. If not longer.

'A visitor, me thinks,' wheezed the woman, looking me up and down. I did the same to her and realised she was dressed in a hideous brown apron over a tatty pink dressing gown and big black boots. 'On a Saturday,' she continued. 'Unexpected, that is. In a good way. Is it me birthday?'

I didn't move a muscle. 'Perhaps,' I mumbled. 'Happy birthday if it is … I'm here to see Mr Hump.'

''Course you is,' nodded the woman. 'On you go then. Me not stands in your way.'

Unfortunately, she already was. Nevertheless, one big breath later and I had managed to shuffle past her whilst avoiding eye contact at all times.

'Mr Hump, it's me,' I cried, trying (and failing) not to raise my voice as I pounded on his door. 'The … um … writer of your book.'

I flinched as something wet and slimy flicked against my neck. Spinning around, I half-expected to find the woman stood right behind me, but I was wrong. She had vanished. Her stench, however, wasn't so quick to disappear.

'Mr Hump!' I yelled. 'Are you in there?'

'Where else would I be?' barked Armitage from somewhere behind the door. 'I told you I … watch what you're doing, you dim-witted dumpling! You nearly sliced my ear off!'

Right on cue, the door swung open.

I held my ground and found myself staring straight into Armitage Hump's sitting room. Or what should have been his sitting room. There was no television or sofa. No ornaments or decorations. Just bare wooden floorboards with a rotten, old writing desk in one corner, a wonky-looking coat stand in the other, and a tall grandfather clock somewhere in between.

Oh, and two men. They were facing each other in the middle of the room.

Sword fighting.

3.'HUMP.'

I looked again.

On closer inspection only one of the men was armed with a sword. He was to my left, dressed entirely in white, including a mask that all but covered his face except for two tiny slits that he could see out of.

The other man was over to my right. Dressed in a black roll-neck sweater and tight trousers (both of which you would struggle to remove without a pair of very sharp scissors), he was much taller than his opponent and incredibly bendy. From the tip of his nose to the toes of his ridiculously pointy shoes, every last bit of him appeared to have been stretched to at least twice its natural length before being twisted inside out. His face was thin, his cheeks were sunken and his eyes were dark and wild. As was his hair. And his eyebrows. Even his eyelashes needed taming a little.

And then we come to the weapon he was fighting with. It wasn't a sword like I had first imagined.

No, it was a golf club.

'Prepare to meet thy maker!' snarled the man in white, lunging forward with his sword raised.

Without missing a beat, the pointy man sashayed smartly to one side like a trained ballet dancer. 'Prepare to meet thy maker?' he repeated, as the blade whizzed past his chest. I recognised his voice immediately. It was Armitage Hump. 'Oh, you mean I'm going to die,' he said matter-of-factly. 'I don't think so somehow, you preposterous prune. I've been in far worse situations than this and lived to tell the tale. I once survived forty-three days in Mrs Goose's wardrobe with nothing to eat or drink. That is, unless you count the mouse droppings. Which I did. I counted them ... and then I ate them! They were a bit chewy, but I've had worse.'

The man in white didn't appear to be listening as he slashed his sword violently from side to side. Armitage dipped, ducked and dodged before eventually diving for cover. To my surprise, he was back on his feet just in time to see the blade slice the minute hand straight off the grandfather clock.

'Hey! That's an antique!' Armitage yelled. 'It's priceless. Or is it worthless? Either way, this needs to stop now before you do one of us some damage. And when I say one of us, what I really mean is me. You can chop your own arm off for all I care!'

With that, Armitage leapt high into the air with his golf club twirling in front of him like a cheerleader's baton. Stood rooted to the spot, the man in white could do nothing but watch in horror as his sword was knocked clean out of his hands.

'Hole in one,' shouted Armitage, upon landing. 'Now, what should I do with you ... um ... what's your name again?'

'Kevin,' mumbled the man in white.

'Of course it is,' nodded Armitage. 'What else would you call your unfriendly neighbourhood ninja? Right, Kevin, I'll give you two choices. You can either feel the pain of my golf club, or you can—'

Without warning, Kevin raced across the room and threw himself at the window. I turned away before the moment of impact, but still heard the uncomfortably loud *smash* of breaking glass, followed by an even more uncomfortable squeal of pain. Sure enough, when I looked again, the man in white had gone.

'First you see him, then you don't.' Wandering across the room, Armitage picked up the sword and tossed it casually out of the man-shaped hole in the window. 'Kevin's bound to come back and get that sooner or later,' he muttered to himself. 'No self-respecting ninja goes anywhere without his weapon.'

'Who was he?' I asked nervously.

'No idea,' shrugged Armitage. 'Up until thirteen days ago I had never even met him. Ever since then, however, he's been trying to cut bits off me at least three times a day.'

'That's terrible,' I said, shaking my head. 'Why would he do that?'

'I thought that would've been obvious,' frowned Armitage. 'Kevin doesn't like me. And he's not the only one. I don't mean to scare you off, but I'm possibly the most disturbingly dislikeable, decidedly disagreeable, downright disgusting person in the whole of Passing Wind. Men and women ... young and old ... thick and thin ... round and square … they all find me irritating. I'm like an itch that can't be stamped on. A pest that can't be scratched.' Armitage stopped suddenly and looked me up and down. 'You're a child,' he remarked, clearly repulsed by what he saw.

'I'm not,' I argued. 'I just look young for my age. It must be all the fresh air I get.'

'I thought you were a writer,' said Armitage suspiciously. 'You don't get much fresh air sat at a desk all day.' Moving swiftly, he swung the golf club and balanced it on the end of my nose. 'No, you look like a child, you speak like a child, and, most important of all, you smell like a child. Both sweet and sour. Very unpleasant on the nostrils.'

'I am not a child,' I said, pushing the club away. 'If anything I'm a teenager. I'm thirteen.'

'Thirteen?' snorted Armitage. 'When I was thirteen I was over seven foot tall. Doesn't your mother feed you properly?'

'Of course she does,' I said. 'And you've never been seven foot tall.'

'I have,' insisted Armitage. 'I've just shrunk a little. It's quite common at my age. My brain's been getting smaller ever since I first got my head trapped in the washing machine. That was an accident. The sixteen other times I got it trapped, however, were all deliberate. Still, enough about me. Let's laugh at you for a bit. Ha! That'll do. Too much laughter always gives me a headache. Right, where were we? Ah, yes, I've two questions for you, child. What's your name? Why are you here? And did you think to bring me any cheese?'

I screwed up my face. 'That's three questions.'

'Don't try and pull the rug out from under my eyebrows,' scowled Armitage. 'Just tell me the truth. Name?'

'Molly.' I hesitated. 'Molly Coddle.'

'Oh, very funny,' groaned Armitage. 'And I suppose my name is Armitage Warbling Cabbage-Patch Hump, isn't it?'

'I don't know,' I shrugged. 'I mean, it could be …'

'Well, yes, it is,' muttered a clearly frustrated Armitage. 'That was a bad example. Listen, stop trying to change the subject, you pesky … erm … subject changer. Why are you here?'

'The book,' I said, trying to avoid eye contact.

'Ah, the book,' repeated Armitage, stroking his chin. 'Is that true or just another of your devious little lies?'

I considered my words carefully before I replied. 'I *would* like to write a book about you.'

'In that case, get cracking,' said Armitage, waving the golf club about his apartment. 'Let's start in here. My natural habitat. As you can see, there's not much to take in. Just the one room.'

I looked around, confused. 'Where do you sleep?'

'On the floor,' replied Armitage.

'So, where do you go to the toilet?' I asked, fearing the worst.

'On the floor,' repeated Armitage.

I tried to lift both feet off the carpet, but failed tragically and almost fell over. 'That's disgusting.'

'You say disgusting, I say unavoidable,' argued Armitage. 'Only number ones, of course. I do my number twos in the garden. Not always my own garden either. Don't pull that face at me. Needs must when money's tighter than a buffalo's belt.'

'I thought you were a famous private detective,' I said.

'*Private famous* detective,' stressed Armitage. 'That's twice you've got it wrong. But, yes, I am.'

'Which means you've solved lots of cases,' I continued. 'How do you get paid?'

'In cheese,' replied Armitage, licking his lips. 'Like you said, Mole, I've solved lots of cases … and I've also eaten lots of cheese!'

'Mole?' I paused, unsure if I had heard correctly. 'It's Molly.'

'It *was* Molly,' grinned Armitage. 'I prefer Mole. It rolls off the tongue better. Less syllables.'

I was about to protest when the door creaked open and in crept the revolting creature I had first met in the hallway.

'Out!' barked Armitage, poking her with his golf club. 'You know the rules, Goose. Knock first before entering.'

The revolting creature that I now knew to be the landlady of Tipsy Towers, Mrs Goose, mumbled something under her breath before shuffling back outside, stopping only to close the door behind her.

A moment later there was a knock.

'Not today, thank you,' shouted Armitage. 'I'm busy.'

'Doing what?' croaked Mrs Goose.

'Lots of things,' Armitage spluttered. 'I'm … um … waxing my underpants … flossing my armpits … brushing my toenails. Whatever it is, Goose, I'm currently unavailable.'

'It's not me who wants you, Army,' replied his landlady. 'You've got yourself another visitor. A real lady. Very la-de-da. Smells nice, too. Not a bit like yours truly.'

Armitage recoiled in horror. 'This visitor you speak of sounds absolutely atrocious,' he said loudly. 'Tell her to go away and don't come back.'

'I'd rather not,' insisted Mrs Goose.

'Why on earth not?' cried Armitage.

The door flew open without warning. 'Cos she's here, ain't she?' said Mrs Goose, poking her head into the apartment. 'She's been stood besides me all the time we've been talking.'

4.'CURSE.'

I watched as a tall, elegant lady with a walking stick crossed the threshold into Armitage Hump's dreadfully dismal apartment.

Mrs Goose was right in her description. Dressed smartly in a long, beige coat over a flowery dress, the lady had a graceful way about her that made her seem completely at odds with her shabby surroundings.

'Get out!' screamed Armitage at the top of his voice. The lady stopped suddenly, unsure whether or not to do as he asked. 'No, not you,' said Armitage, pointing over her shoulder with the golf club. 'I was talking to the Goose. I've already looked at her four times this morning … and that's four times too many for anybody to stomach!'

'You knows wheres to finds me if you needs me,' wheezed Mrs Goose, as she closed the door behind her.

'Yes, in the sewer with the rest of the rodents,' remarked Armitage, loud enough for his landlady to hear. At the same time he turned to face the new arrival. 'Take a seat and we can begin,' he said, gesturing around the room.

The lady looked around. 'Sorry … there's not … I can't

24

seem to find a chair.'

'Who said anything about a chair?' frowned Armitage. 'What's wrong with the floor?'

'There's *a lot* wrong with the floor,' muttered the lady under her breath.

'Just avoid the damp patches,' shrugged Armitage. 'It's no big deal.'

'Maybe not to you, but I think I'd rather stand,' insisted the lady, leaning on her walking stick. 'These are troublesome times, Mr Hump, so I'll get straight to the point. What I'm about to tell you is simply horrific. My name is Constance Snoot—'

'You have my deepest sympathy,' said Armitage. 'You could always change it, I suppose. Something like Marjory Stiff-Neck would suit you better. Or Hilda Wildebeest.'

Constance glared at Armitage for what seemed like an age. 'My name is not the problem,' she said eventually.

'If you say so,' Armitage smirked. 'Okay, what is then? Let me guess. Your face? Your clothes? No, I've got it. It's your hair, isn't it? Who knew the vegetable patch look was in fashion this season? Certainly not me. Which gardener did you get to grow it for you?'

'Armitage!' I cried out. 'That's really rude.'

Shifting her gaze, Constance appeared to notice me for the first time. 'Oh, I didn't realise we had company,' she said, turning her nose up. 'And such small company at that.'

'She's just leaving,' said Armitage.

'I am not,' I said stubbornly.

'Okay, she's *not* just leaving,' muttered Armitage. 'Don't

let her put you off, though. She's very easy to ignore. If anything, she's like a belly button. Completely pointless.'

'This was clearly a mistake,' said Constance, shaking her head as she turned towards the door. 'I don't know what the relationship is between you two, but I seem to have wandered into a battlefield. I should probably come back later.'

'Yes, you probably should,' nodded Armitage.

'No, you definitely shouldn't!' Without thinking, I hurried across the apartment and blocked the door. 'You can't go,' I said. 'Please. Armitage doesn't mean it. He's had a nasty shock, that's all. There was a man in the apartment … a ninja … Kevin. He had a sword … and then he jumped out of the window!'

'Gosh, that sounds truly frightful,' Constance gasped. 'At least you were here to come to his aid. You seem very young to be his assistant, though—'

'Mole is not my assistant!' roared Armitage. 'I work alone. I fly solo. Independently of all others. No, Mole's only here because she's—'

'Writing a book,' I said, finishing his sentence. 'The … erm … Curious Cases of Armitage Hump.'

'That's a rubbish name,' Armitage blurted out. 'If nothing else, it doesn't make sense. This apartment is a case-free zone. There's not a suitcase, briefcase or bookcase in sight.'

Constance turned to me, confused. 'Is he being deliberately stupid?'

'It's hard to tell,' I replied honestly. 'I am writing a book, though,' I added, not quite so honestly.

'If you're struggling for a title then I think I can help,' said Constance. 'How about ... The Curse of Crooked Elbow?'

'How about ... not on your kneecaps!' groaned Armitage. 'I don't even live in Crooked Elbow for a start. And I've not been cursed.'

'No, but I have,' remarked Constance.

The apartment fell silent.

'Have you really?' Armitage arched one of his bushy eyebrows. 'I like the sound of that. Explain yourself, Miss Snot.'

'Snoot,' said Constance, correcting him.

'Snoot to you too,' replied Armitage, pulling a face at his visitor. 'Still, all insults aside, do go on. I'm waiting.'

Constance took a deep breath. 'For the past few weeks I've been living in Drab House on the outskirts of Crooked Elbow,' she began. 'It's the home of my aunt and uncle, Cynthia and Wilfred Drabble. They've gone skiing so I offered to house sit for them whilst they're away.'

Opening his mouth as wide as possible, Armitage yawned loudly. 'Wake me up when things get interesting,' he grumbled.

'I was just giving you some back story, you beastly brute!' Constance raised her walking stick as if she were about to hit him, before lowering it a moment later. 'Apologies,' she said calmly. 'I'm afraid the curse has knocked me completely cock-a-hoop. Let me start again. I'm a nice person, Mr Hump. Polite and well-mannered. Very friendly. I'm not one for making enemies and yet somebody has clearly taken offence to something I've either said or done. Now they want to make me suffer. And that's why they've burdened me with this dreaded curse!'

Constance visibly shivered as she glanced over her shoulder.

'Take your time,' I said.

'Don't you dare!' cried Armitage. 'If anything, hurry up. Jump straight to the juicy bits. You know, where you turn into a werewolf and feast on the flesh of the elderly.'

'That is not my curse,' said Constance sadly. 'No, to my despair I have been blighted with a lifetime of sleepwrecking.'

'Sleepwrecking?' I screwed up my face. 'Don't you mean sleepwalking?'

'If I meant sleepwalking, I would've said sleepwalking,' shot back Constance. 'Sleepwrecking is something else entirely.'

'Yes, sleepwrecking is something else entirely,' repeated Armitage, sticking his tongue out at me. 'It's when you … um … wreck things in your sleep.'

'That's it exactly,' nodded Constance. 'I've no recollection of what I do when I leave the house in the middle of the night and then walk the streets of Crooked Elbow. Not until the next day, at least. That's when I see the broken windows … the trampled flowerbeds … the dented cars … the rubbish strewn here, there and everywhere. Quite simply, it's a trail of destruction. And there's no way I can stop myself from doing it.'

'You could always hide the door key,' I suggested. 'That way you can't get out of the house.'

'I tried that,' replied Constance. 'I hid it behind the fireplace … but then I found it whilst I was asleep!'

'Try swallowing it,' said Armitage. 'Or stick it up your nose. It's big enough.'

'You're not taking me seriously, Mr Hump.' With a shaky hand, Constance removed a handkerchief from her coat pocket and began to dab her eyes. 'You think this is one big joke,' she sobbed. 'Well, it's not. It's ruining my life.'

'I know the feeling,' muttered Armitage under his breath. 'Oh, what do *you* want?'

He was talking to me. Not only had I edged closer to him, but now I was trying to whisper in his ear.

'I think you've upset her,' I pointed out.

'Oh, I should've guessed it'd be my fault,' moaned Armitage.

'Go and comfort her,' I said. 'Put an arm around her shoulder … tell her it'll be okay.'

Armitage just snorted. 'I'm not really a touchy-feely kind of person. I'm more hands off than hands on.'

'You've got to do something,' I said, shoving him in the back. 'She's getting louder. If you're not careful Mrs Goose will be in to see what all the fuss is about.'

The thought of that seemed to spur Armitage into action. Tip-toeing across the room, he held his golf club at arm's length and used it to pat Constance on the shoulder. 'There, there, Miss Snot,' he said awkwardly. 'There's no need to make such a horrendous racket. Besides, you don't look your best when you're crying. Quite hideous actually. Like a warthog with something sharp stuck in its throat.'

Miraculously, Armitage's words of *comfort* seemed to do the trick.

'I'm fine,' said Constance, pushing the golf club away. 'Honestly. It's just … can you imagine how it feels when everyone you know thinks you're a horrible, horrible person?'

'Yes, obviously,' replied Armitage, without missing a beat. 'That's my life.'

'Then surely you can help me, Mr Hump,' Constance pleaded. 'You're my last resort. My only hope. My … what's the matter now?'

'Don't mind me, Miss Snot.' Staring up at the ceiling, Armitage started to spin around on the spot. 'I'm still listening,' he insisted. 'Most of the time. The rest of the time I'm looking for …' He stopped suddenly as a drop of water fell from a slight crack and landed on his forehead. 'Ah, bullseye,' Armitage cried.

'You've got a leak,' I said, following his gaze. 'Do you know where it's coming from?'

'Those not-so delightful Darlings upstairs,' revealed Armitage, gesturing rudely at the apartment above. 'Twice a day – at ten in the morning and three in the afternoon – they play their … *noise* so loud that it makes their toilet shake. I would call it music, but then music shouldn't sound like a motorcycle with a squirrel stuck in its exhaust.'

'Why don't you put a bucket down?' I said.

'Why in the wild world of weirdness would I want to put a bucket down?' With that, Armitage began to remove his clothing. Thankfully, he stopped when he reached his underpants. 'Like I said before, don't mind me.'

'What are you doing?' I asked nervously.

'Taking a shower, of course.' Standing under the leak, Armitage let the drips from the ceiling splatter against his forehead. 'That's better,' he said. 'I've not had a wash in days. Yes, I know I've got visitors, but that doesn't mean I should pass up the opportunity. Do continue, Miss Snot. You were telling us about this ridiculous curse of yours—'

'It is not ridiculous!' barked Constance. 'It's very upsetting. I was at the Cold Crooked Carnival when Madame Isabella first broke it to me. She's a fortune teller. She saw it in my tea leaves. The sleepwrecking started the very same night and things have never been the same again.' Constance slowly shook her head. 'You are listening, aren't you, Mr Hump?'

'Who? Me? Unfortunately so,' said Armitage, bending over so he could clean the dirt out from between his toes. 'Very well, Miss Snot, I've heard your story and I'm pleased it's over. What I don't understand, however, is what you want me to do?'

'I thought that would've been obvious,' replied Constance brusquely. 'I want you to find out who it was that cursed me and then get them to remove it. And I want you to start immediately.'

'Immediately?' Armitage wiped the water from his eyes. 'Can't you see I'm taking a shower?'

'I can see you're standing under a drip in the ceiling,' remarked Constance. 'Start after that then. As soon as possible.'

'Or maybe just as soon as *not* possible,' argued Armitage.

'I've got things to do, Miss Snot. Don't you know that the Stinking Wedge is in Crooked Elbow?'

The look on Constance's face seemed to suggest she didn't. And she wasn't the only.

'What's the Stinking Wedge?' I asked.

Armitage threw his arms up in despair. 'Don't they teach you anything in school these days? The Stinking Wedge is only the most famous cheese in the history of cheese. And now it's on display at Mysterious Melvin's Museum of Mind-Bending Marvels for one day and one day only.'

'It sounds … lovely,' I lied.

'It is,' nodded Armitage. 'Come tomorrow, I can admire its beauty and breathe in its powerfully pungent aroma. Even experienced cheese sniffers have been known to pass out it reeks so bad. Oh, I've waited years for such an opportunity so there's no way I can pass it up … no, stop that, Miss Snot! Stop that right now! I'm warning you!'

I turned to Constance, surprised to see that she had, once again, begun to weep uncontrollably.

'This isn't fair,' moaned Armitage, as the music faded and the drips from the ceiling began to dry up. 'I only wanted to get up close and personal to the Stinking Wedge … arrggghhh! Have it your way, Miss Snot. You win. I'll do it. I'll take the case and then everybody will be happy. Everybody except me.' Armitage wrapped his arms around his half-naked body. 'Now, pass me my trousers, Mole,' he demanded, pointing rudely at the pile of clothes he had tossed to one side. 'If I'm going to solve the curse of Crooked Elbow then I'd rather not do it in the nude!'

5.'WHEELS.'

Without bothering to dry himself, Armitage started to get dressed.

'That's better,' he said, pulling on his jumper. 'Nothing like a good shower.'

'Yes, *that* was nothing like a good shower,' I remarked.

An exasperated Constance Snoot seemed to have heard enough. 'Right, I think we can all agree that I've stayed far too long in this filthy flea-pit,' she muttered, turning towards the door. 'So long, Mr Hump. I hope to see you at Drab House before the morning is out. Oh, I almost forgot. How would you like to be paid?'

'In cheese,' replied Armitage, as he squeezed into his trousers. 'I'm not expecting anything as revoltingly grand as the Stinking Wedge, of course. The smellier the better, though. Nice and stinky.'

Constance's brow began to furrow. 'You'd like me to pay you in cheese?'

'No, not cheese,' I said hastily. 'In money … please.'

Armitage hesitated for a moment. 'Okay, money,' he shrugged. 'Money to buy cheese.'

DAVID CODD

'No, money to fix that leak,' I said, pointing up at the ceiling. 'Or to buy you a bed … or a toilet … or a new carpet. The list is endless.'

Reaching into her handbag, Constance removed her purse. 'How about five hundred up front and then a hundred for every day there after?'

'Whatever,' mumbled Armitage. 'I'm no longer listening … without cheese my life means nothing.'

Constance ignored him and chose, instead, to hand me a bundle of notes.

'That's perfect,' I said, tucking them into my back pocket. 'Thank you. We'll start immediately. I promise.'

'We?' scowled Armitage, stretching a sock over his dripping toes. '*I'll* start immediately. You, however, Mole, can go and spend that money on a giant sponge.'

I screwed up my face. 'A sponge?'

'You can stick it in your mouth,' explained Armitage. 'If nothing else it'll stop you from talking. Whilst you're at it you might want to get yourself a bucket as well. You can put that over your head. It'll be a great improvement.'

'Don't worry about me,' said Constance, hurrying towards the door. 'I can see myself out.'

Sure enough, a moment later, she had gone.

'Do you have to be so rude?' I asked, scowling at Armitage.

'I don't have to be – I *love* to be,' he replied. 'If you don't like it you can always follow Miss Snot and leave me in peace. Oh, please say you don't like it.'

I could feel my blood beginning to boil. Armitage Hump was the meanest, foulest, most disgustingly awkward person

I had ever met. And yet …

'Are you feeling okay?' I took a step back as Armitage began to violently shake from head to toe. Before I knew it, his face was burning up as sweat started to trickle down his forehead. If anything, he looked like a human volcano ready to explode.

'No, I am not okay!' Armitage boomed. The shaking stopped without warning, only to be replaced by a sudden burst of bouncing up and down on the spot. 'This is what I like to call a massive mind melt,' he yelled. 'A brain-blast. A hazardous head-pop. As much as I was looking forward to sniffing the Stinking Wedge, the curse of Crooked Elbow is a once in a lifetime occurrence.'

'Is it?' I said.

'It is if I say it is,' insisted Armitage. 'Truth is, Mole, I've been bored. Bored stiff. As bored as a balloon that's missing its ball. An *oon*. That's all I've become. No, as far as I'm concerned Miss Snot and her sleepwrecking is the light at the end of my particular boredom tunnel.'

Without another word, he ran straight past me as he left the apartment.

'Where are you going?' I called out.

'Crooked Elbow, of course,' Armitage replied. 'Drab House here I come.'

His voice had already begun to fade into the distance when I came to a decision. 'Wait! Don't leave me here on my … oof!'

I was out the door and halfway across the hallway when I crashed into something small and unpleasant.

Also known as Mrs Goose.

'Me not thinks we've been properly introduced,' she wheezed, holding out a wrinkly hand for me to shake.

'This is Emily Wires-Crossed,' said Armitage, squeezing between us.

'That's not my name,' I argued.

'Be quiet, Miss Wires-Crossed!' snapped Armitage. 'Never tell the Goose your real name. Don't even tell her your shoe size. She'll only use it against you. That's what she's like. She's not to be trusted. She's—'

'Still here.' Mrs Goose's eyes were virtually popping out of their sockets as she gave me a quick once over. 'Oh, she's a pretty one alright, Army. Has she got a price?'

'Nothing you could afford,' growled Armitage. 'Besides, she's not for sale. Not to you, anyway. You'd probably try and eat her.'

'Don't be like that,' said Mrs Goose, grinning wickedly as she licked the spit off her dry lips. 'You still owes me this month's rent. And now we can adds a broken window to that as well. Maybe, 'cos me is mostly feeling generous, we could always comes to an … arrangement.'

'Arrangement?' Armitage shook a fist at his landlady. 'The only thing you'll be arranging is your teeth … and that's once I've accidentally knocked them out on purpose with a sledgehammer!'

'Wouldn't bothers me if you did.' Thrusting her fingers into her mouth, Mrs Goose pulled out a full set of dentures. 'They're falsies,' she mumbled.

'That doesn't mean you shouldn't clean them once in a

while,' said Armitage, backing away from her. 'Your breath's so rancid it's burning a hole in my eyeballs. Come now, Miss Wires-Crossed,' he said, urging me to follow him. 'Let's skedaddle quick sharpish before this old gutwrencher gets under our fingernails and poisons our blood.'

Mrs Goose waited until she had put her teeth back in before she spoke again. 'Aren't you forgetting something, Army? What abouts me rent?'

'It's coming,' Armitage insisted.

'It's always coming,' moaned Mrs Goose.

'And if you stay alive long enough it might just arrive!' With that, Armitage barged past his landlady and stormed out of Tipsy Towers.

'Me'll knit you a scarf, Army,' said Mrs Goose, as she shuffled down the steps towards the basement. 'A *long* scarf. Long enough to keep your toes warm when me cuts off your power.'

I took one last look at the wizened, old landlady before she disappeared from view. Her head may have vanished, but one of her twisted fingers was still hovering above the surface, beckoning me to join her. I shivered at the thought of it. Okay, so Armitage Hump wasn't exactly to everyone's taste, but the prospect of a morning spent in the company of the gruesome Goose was enough to make my skin crawl.

'I don't think I like her,' I said, once I'd finally caught up with Armitage.

'There's no thinking about it!' he roared back at me. 'You *don't* like her! Nobody does! Goose is slipperier than a snake on a jelly bus. Quite simply, she's the most sickening snotgoblin that has ever set foot on the planet. Now, try and forget about her whilst we concentrate on the job at hand.'

'Which is?' I wondered.

'To get my wheels.' With his head down, Armitage hopped off the pavement and marched straight across a busy road without looking. Cars whizzed by at speed, beeping their horns as they swerved to avoid him. I, meanwhile, chose the sensible option and waited for a gap in the traffic before I raced after him. I had watched him turn down a narrow side street, but when I got there he was nowhere to be seen. I dropped my speed and began to walk. Armitage seemed to have blended into the background, a background that consisted of nothing but bare brick walls and industrial-size dustbins.

The sound of screeching tyres made me spin sharply on the spot. To my surprise, a dark car had also turned down the side street. I was even more surprised when it started to accelerate. Surely it was going too fast for somewhere so narrow. I blinked once … twice … three times, but the car was still coming.

Was it my imagination, or was it driving straight at me?

A second later and I knew the answer.

It *wasn't* my imagination.

Staggering backwards, I was about to scream in horror when Armitage stepped out from the shadows. He held up his hand, but the car seemed to increase its speed. Then he held up his other hand and the same thing happened again. The car sped up even more.

Without a second thought, I threw myself to one side,

landing awkwardly amongst the rubbish bags and cardboard boxes that lined the edges of the street. At the same time I heard the loudest *screech* of all. Rolling over, I was relieved to see that Armitage hadn't been flattened like I had feared. No, quite incredibly, he was still stood on the very same spot. The car, meanwhile, was only inches from his toes.

'Enjoying yourself down there, Mole?' Armitage laughed at me.

I had barely climbed to my feet when a small, stocky woman in a long, black coat climbed out of the car. Without saying a word, she tossed a set of keys into the air before marching off in the opposite direction.

'See you in two days,' shouted Armitage, catching the keys one-handed.

'Who was she?' I wondered.

'How am I supposed to know?' shrugged Armitage. 'We car share, that's all. She uses it for work and then I have it at the weekend. Doesn't mean we have to be friends, does it?'

I wasn't quite sure if Armitage was telling the truth. I was even less convinced when I took a proper look at the car. 'Isn't that a—?'

'Hearse,' finished Armitage, as he pulled open the door.

I screwed up my face. 'But aren't they used for—?'

'Funerals,' finished Armitage for a second time. Ducking his head, he shuffled into the driver's seat. 'Don't look so worried, Mole. It's not as if she's left any dead bodies in the back, is it?' Armitage hesitated. 'I mean, she hasn't, has she? Because she has before. On more than one occasion. Bit embarrassing really. Especially the time I failed to notice.

One sharp turn later and the coffin flew out the back and split in two. What a sight that was!'

'Too much information.' I reluctantly made my way around to the passenger side door. 'You can drive, can't you?' I asked warily.

'How dare you!' shot back Armitage. 'I did my test years ago. Well … I did *a* test. It could have been a spelling test for all I know. Still, let's not dwell on the bad old days. Get in now or I'll take you back to Tipsy Towers and the ghastly Goose!'

With the threat ringing in my ears, I flung open the door and climbed into the hearse.

'Cold Crooked Carnival here we come,' announced Armitage.

'I thought we were going to meet Constance Snoot at Drab House,' I said.

'We were … but now we're not,' replied Armitage. 'My mind is like my underpants, Mole. I change it at least once a month. And today's that lucky day. It was Madame Isabella who told Concrete Snot that she had been cursed so let's go and quiz her. Believe me, Mole, I won't stop until I find out who cast that curse. Even if it breaks me in two.'

'Sounds dangerous,' I said, pulling on my seat belt.

'Let's hope so.' Armitage turned the key and the hearse grumbled into life. 'Because if it wasn't dangerous then it wouldn't be worth doing now, would it?'

6.'QUEUE.'

The journey from Passing Wind to the Cold Crooked Carnival was neither short nor sweet.

It *was*, however, excruciatingly terrifying.

In typical Armitage Hump fashion, his driving was much like his general behaviour – erratic. If he wasn't stalling, braking too hard or swerving wildly, then he was picking thick clumps of wax out of his ears and flicking them over his shoulder. I wanted to say something, but chose, instead, to sit in silence with my eyes half-closed and my fingers clenched tightly on the seat beneath me. This wasn't a car journey; this was a roller-coaster ride. Still, at least we hadn't quite managed to loop-the-loop.

Not yet, anyway …

'Driving's so boring,' moaned Armitage, as he carelessly spun the steering wheel. 'Why don't you ask me a question, Mole? Anything you want. You can use it in your book.'

I took a breath whilst I built up the courage to speak. 'What did you do before you became a famous private … a *private* famous detective?'

'What did I do?' Armitage snorted. 'What *didn't* I do!

I've had more jobs than you've had bad haircuts. One hundred and sixty-three to be precise. From sewer inspecting to worm-bothering, I've done the lot,' he said proudly.

'Worm-bothering?' I repeated. 'What's that?'

Armitage squirmed in his seat. 'I'd rather not say. I still have nightmares about it now.'

'Oh, please tell me,' I said, trying not to laugh. 'It sounds really ... stop!'

To my surprise, Armitage did as I asked and slammed on the brakes.

'What's wrong?' he barked. 'You're not going to be sick, are you? If so, try and swallow it before it escapes from your mouth—'

'No, I'm not going to be sick.' I gestured out of the window at two people – a man and a woman – who were walking hand-in-hand on the opposite side of the road.

'Don't point,' snapped Armitage. 'It's rude. On second thoughts, point away. In fact, I think I'll join you. Let's see who we can offend.'

'They're my parents,' I said, opening the hearse door. 'I should run over and speak to them. Tell them where I'm going. And, more importantly, who I'm going there with.'

'Don't you move a muscle, Mole!' Reaching over, Armitage slammed the door before I could get out. 'Leave this to me. I'll talk to them.'

I screwed up my face. 'I didn't think you liked talking to people.'

'I don't,' frowned Armitage. 'The thought of it is enough to make my bottom wobble. Nevertheless, we all have to do things we don't like from time to time. Especially if I'm going to get my book.'

Armitage was already halfway out the door by the time I spoke again. 'My parents are quite protective of me. You're not going to do anything … weird, are you?'

'Weird? Me?' he grinned. 'Strange perhaps. Odd quite possibly. But not weird.'

I covered my eyes as Armitage rushed across the road, but still found myself peeking through the gaps in my fingers. Unsurprisingly, my mum jumped in horror and my dad leapt back as Armitage almost charged straight into them. They looked shocked, maybe even a little scared. I was all set to hurry to their rescue when, right on cue, my dad began to smile and my mum laughed out loud. Next thing I knew my dad was shaking Armitage by the hand, whilst my mum went one step further and kissed him on the cheek.

It was only when Armitage had returned to the hearse that I finally removed my hands.

'Don't look so scared, Mole,' he said, starting the engine. 'We don't want them to think you're having a rotten time, do we?'

I both waved and smiled as the hearse stuttered into life and we drove past my parents. 'What did you say to them?' I asked, fearing the worst.

'The truth, the truth, and nothing but the truth,' revealed Armitage. 'I told them who I was and where I was going. I also told them that you were coming with me.'

'And they agreed?' I said, dumbfounded.

'Naturally,' nodded Armitage. 'But then they didn't

really have a choice, did they? I am Armitage Hump, after all. You never told me they were massive fans of mine.'

'I didn't know they were,' I shrugged.

'Well, you do now,' said Armitage. 'They told me not to bring you home until we'd finished in Crooked Elbow. They also said what a great thrill it would be for you to help me with one of my cases. That bit, of course, was a lie. You won't be helping me. The best we can hope is that you don't get under my feet. Still, at least your parents won't be ringing the police any time soon. I'd hate to get arrested for kidnapping … again.'

My mouth fell open. And that was how it stayed until we finally pulled up at the gates to the Cold Crooked Carnival.

We had arrived. And I was still alive. Both of which had seemed highly unlikely when we had first set off.

Quite simply, the Cold Crooked Carnival was a huge field full of tents, stalls and food stands (not to mention the odd cow or four). Admission was free, which was a huge relief seeing as Armitage marched straight past the entrance without even breaking stride.

'This looks interesting,' I said, following him through the damp grass.

'Does it?' Armitage grumbled. 'There are far too many pimples here for my liking.'

'Pimples?' I said, confused.

'Simple people,' explained Armitage. 'And too many pimples means too many smells. I've already detected wet dog twinned with baby sick mixed with rotten eggs blended with fish paste … and that's only in one nostril!'

'That might just be you,' I muttered under my breath.

'True,' agreed Armitage. 'Right, keep your eyes peeled for any sign of this fortune teller, Mole. She's probably hiding somewhere so I doubt you'll spot her before—'

'There!' Hurrying forward, I stopped at a large, wooden sign covered in white paint.

Madame Isabella, Fortune Teller.

'What gave it away?' said Armitage, rolling his eyes at me. 'Was it the sign with Madame Isabella written on it? Or was it the sign with Madame Isabella written on it?'

'You're not funny,' I moaned.

'And neither is that!' Armitage pointed at the long line of people beside the wooden sign. 'What is it exactly?'

'A queue,' I said. 'I'm guessing that everybody standing here wants their fortunes read.'

'And I'm guessing that nobody else in this queue is anywhere near as important as me,' remarked Armitage loudly. 'You're certainly not,' he said, pushing past a man who was stood in front of us. That would've been bad enough, but Armitage hadn't quite finished yet. 'Or you,' he said, squeezing past another. 'Or you ... definitely not you ... you're not even facing the right way ...'

I knew it was the wrong thing to do, but that didn't stop me from following Armitage all the way to the front of the queue.

'Ah, that's better,' he said, rubbing his hands together. 'You don't think any of these pimples will mind someone as special as me going first, do you?'

'Yes, I think they might,' I said, shaking my head in disbelief. 'Starting with him …'

Armitage was about to speak when two huge hands grabbed him by the shoulders and spun him around.

'You pushed in,' grunted a big brute of a man with a bulging forehead and tiny eyes.

'Correct,' nodded Armitage. 'I was hoping you wouldn't notice, but never mind. What do you want? An autograph? A photograph? Surely not a kiss and a cuddle?'

'I want you to move,' said the man gruffly.

'Move?' Armitage looked down at his feet and frowned. 'Do you mean dance? Or just shuffle about a bit?'

'I want you to move to the back,' the man insisted.

'We should probably do as he says,' I whispered.

'We shall do no such thing!' cried Armitage, puffing out his chest. 'There's no need to get your pigtails in a panic about this great goon, Mole. I mean, what's he going to do? It's not as if he can just lift me up and toss me to one side like an old carrot!'

It took four seconds for Armitage's words to wrestle their way into the big brute's skull and another three before they finally filtered into his brain. On the eighth second he raised Armitage above his head and threw him as far as he could in the opposite direction. The rest of the queue cheered as the detective flew through the air. I looked away, but still heard a dull *splat* followed by a series of moans and groans.

'Are you okay?' I asked, wandering over to where he had landed.

'Why wouldn't I be?' Armitage was laid flat on his stomach with his face pressed into the dirt. 'I quite enjoyed it actually,' he muttered.

'Of course you did,' I said, trying not to grin.

Scrambling to his feet, Armitage frantically scratched his head as he tried to get his bearings. 'Where are we again?' he mumbled.

I nodded towards the wooden sign. Not only were we right back where we had first started – at the rear of the queue – but now even more people had joined and we were further back than before.

'This time we should probably wait our turn like everybody else,' I suggested.

'Have it your way,' said Armitage grumpily. 'Be warned, though. I will literally explode with frustration if it takes us more than thirty-six minutes to get to the front …'

Thirty-seven.

That's how long it took. Armitage, as you can probably guess, didn't explode. He did, however, refuse to stand patiently and insisted, instead, on passing the time as bizarrely as you can possibly imagine. In the space of thirty-seven minutes he managed to fall asleep, wake up, fall asleep again, trip over his own feet, trip over someone else's feet, wipe his face on the same person's jacket and then get covered in bird poo. Twice.

'Well, that was eventful,' I said, shaking my head at Armitage as he pressed his nose up to the red velvet curtain at the entrance to Madame Isabella's tent.

'Was it? I didn't realise,' he said awkwardly. 'What happens now?'

'I think we have to wait to be invited in,' I said.

'Yes, that's what I thought too.' With that, Armitage slipped through the curtain. I tried to grab him before he disappeared, but only succeeded in stumbling forward myself. Before I could regain my balance, I, too, was inside the tent.

The only light in there was coming from a single candle in the centre of a small, circular table. There were two chairs on either side of it, one of which was occupied by a small, frail-looking woman. Hunched over, her entire face was hidden by a thick mass of straggly black curls. Despite the cold, she was dressed in nothing but a white flowy dress that dragged along the grass beneath her feet. Her *bare* feet. Wow! This woman was clearly tougher than she looked.

'My name is Madame Isabella, fortune teller,' the woman whispered. 'And you are … no, it cannot be!' Madame Isabella leapt up off her chair. 'Never in all my days,' she wailed. 'Something so bleak … so joyless … as dark as the eye of a storm …'

'Stop it, you're flattering me,' said Armitage. 'We are in something of a hurry, though, so if you can just answer a few questions … oh, what's the matter now?'

'Not what – who!' cried the fortune teller, pointing with both hands at the man in front of her. 'And when I say who, what I really mean is … you!'

And, with that, Madame Isabella did something that none of us had been expecting.

She started to scream.

7.'MAGIC.'

There were a number of things we could've done when the screaming started.

We could've left the tent. We could've asked Madame Isabella to stop. We could even have put our hands over our ears until she ran out of breath. What we shouldn't have done, however, was start to scream as well. And yet one of us did exactly that.

And that *one of us* wasn't me.

Throwing back his head, Armitage opened his mouth as wide as was humanly possible and let rip with an almighty holler that, somehow, managed to shake the tent to the point of collapsing.

A bewildered Madame Isabella instantly fell silent. 'What are you doing?' she asked.

To my relief, Armitage stopped screaming too. 'You tell me,' he replied. 'You're the fortune teller.'

'That's not how this works,' insisted Madame Isabella. 'Why were you screaming?'

'Because you were,' admitted Armitage. 'And who knew that it was such fun? Now, would you mind if I started again?'

'Certainly not,' said Madame Isabella hastily. 'I wasn't screaming for fun – I was screaming because of … you!'

'I'm not that ugly,' grumbled Armitage. 'Maybe a bit ugly. Moderately ugly. Surely not Mrs Goose ugly, though.'

'I wouldn't know,' remarked Madame Isabella. Lifting a bony hand, she swept her hair to one side. I turned away at the sight that greeted me. Then I turned back for another look. Just to be sure.

Yes, I was right first time. Madame Isabella was missing something from her face. No, make that two things.

Her eyes.

'As you can see, I cannot,' said the fortune teller, her long fingernails jabbing at the two black holes that disappeared into her skull. 'Perhaps you would like to introduce yourself so we can begin the reading.'

'If I must,' sighed Armitage. 'My name is Cedric Parsley-Thyme—'

'That's not true,' said Madame Isabella, without missing a beat.

'Correct,' Armitage grinned. 'I was just testing you. I'm actually Armitage Hump, the private famous detective.'

'Ah, that's more like it,' nodded Madame Isabella, as she finally sat back down again. 'So, you're Armitage Hump—'

'That's incredible,' Armitage blurted out. 'How did you know?'

'You just told her,' I said. 'About a second ago. You can't have forgotten already.'

Armitage pulled a face at me. 'A mind as powerful as mine never forgets to … erm … remember to … um …

what were we talking about?'

'I heard you were coming, Mr Armitage Hump,' said Madame Isabella, her hands twirling above her head. 'There were strong rumours on the psychic grapevine. I had no idea, however, that you had such a dark soul.'

'That's just dirt,' insisted Armitage. 'I'll wipe it off before the end of the day. Which day, however, is anybody's guess.'

'No, it's more than that,' said Madame Isabella. 'There's a cloud that hangs over you …'

'There's a cloud hanging over *everyone* in Crooked Elbow,' grumbled Armitage. 'Not that I'm complaining. It's so grim and gloomy here I might even start coming on holiday.'

'You are lonely,' continued Madame Isabella. 'You have nothing and no one.'

'I've got Mole,' replied Armitage to my surprise.

Madame Isabella hesitated. 'You have a … pet mole?'

'Well, she's more of a pest than a pet,' shrugged Armitage. 'But she is writing a book about me.'

'You have a mole who can write?' Madame Isabella recoiled in horror. 'This is worse than I imagined.'

'No, *you're* worse than I imagined,' remarked Armitage. 'And I wasn't imagining anything that great to begin with. Right, let's start again, shall we? I don't want my fortune read, but I do want information.'

'Information I can do.' A smiling Madame Isabella seemed to relax a little as she rubbed her hands together. 'Cross my palm with silver and my lips might loosen enough for me to spill the beans.'

'That sounds disgusting!' cried Armitage. 'What are you talking about?'

'Give me some money and I'll tell you what you need to know,' explained Madame Isabella bluntly.

'Money … okay … this is awkward.' Armitage turned towards me. 'Mole, give the sour old crone some money, will you?'

'Mole!' Madame Isabella leapt up off her chair for a second time. 'You brought your pet mole to my tent!'

'She is not my pet!' blasted Armitage. 'She is a child. Which, yes, I know, is worse than any pet. Right, Mole … money … now.'

I peeled off two notes from the bundle that Constance Snoot had given me and passed them to Armitage.

'There you go,' he said, stuffing them into the fortune teller's hands. 'Don't spend it all at once. In fact …'

Armitage moved quickly and tried to snatch one of the notes back from Madame Isabella's grasp before she could close her hand. Unfortunately, he didn't move quickly enough.

'Ouch!' he cried out. 'That's my finger you've just crushed!'

'I know,' said Madame Isabella. 'But why was it tickling my palm?'

'No reason,' lied Armitage. 'I … erm … just wanted to hold hands. I'm nice like that.'

'No, you're not,' Madame Isabella argued. 'We've already established that. Now, time is money and unless you want to give me a little more I suggest you hurry up and ask—'

'What do you know about Concrete Snot?' blurted out Armitage.

'Constance Snoot,' I said, correcting him.

'Constance Snoot.' Madame Isabella pressed her forefinger to the side of her head. 'Ah, yes, I remember her clearly,' she said quietly. 'She wanted me to read her fortune. She thought it would be fun.'

'Not at your prices,' moaned Armitage.

'I felt it when she entered the tent,' Madame Isabella continued. 'It was wrapped around her body, squeezing her tight like an angry blanket. Miss Snoot had been cursed.'

'Who by?' asked Armitage.

'That I do not know,' admitted Madame Isabella, 'but the power that came from her, the heavy presence, seemed to suggest that it was a witch or a wizard who had first cast it.'

'Witch or wizard?' snorted Armitage. 'You don't really believe all that hocus pocus nonsense, do you?'

'Of course,' said Madame Isabella. 'Magic is my life. There are magical beings all over Crooked Elbow, but most people simply choose to ignore them. Perhaps they are scared. Like you.'

'I'm not scared of anything,' insisted Armitage. 'Only mirrors. Oh, and moustaches. And mushrooms. And molehills. And mouthwash. And ... would you like me to move on to any other letters in the alphabet now?'

'We're here to help Miss Snoot,' I said, reminding Armitage in case he had forgotten. 'We need to get her curse lifted so she can live a normal life.'

'That is not something you can do,' remarked Madame

Isabella, shaking her head. 'Miss Snoot will be at the mercy of this curse for the rest of her days. Unless …'

'Unless what?' I said.

'Unless the person who first cast it is willing to remove it themselves,' Madame Isabella replied. 'You would need to find them first, of course. And that won't be easy. Witches and wizards can hide perfectly well in plain sight. Sometimes it is those you least suspect who …' Madame Isabella stopped without warning. 'Your time is up,' she announced, turning her back on us. 'I would like you to leave now.'

'I would like me to leave now as well,' said Armitage. 'But then I never wanted to come here in the first place.'

We exited the tent soon after. To my surprise, the queue was even longer than when we had entered.

'Did you see it?' asked Armitage, once we were out of earshot.

I shrugged. 'See what?'

'The note,' Armitage explained. 'On Madame Isabella's table. She was staring at it when we first walked in. Her lips were even moving as if she was reading it. She didn't want us to see what it said so she turned it over.'

'Really?' I frowned, not convinced in the slightest. 'Why would anybody send Madame Isabella a note if she can't see? Unless—'

'She's not really blind,' grinned Armitage, patting me firmly on the forehead as he finished my sentence. 'Well done, Mole. Maybe I was wrong about you. Maybe you're not the stupidest person in Passing Wind, after all. Just the second stupidest.'

I gritted my teeth and resisted the urge to bite back. 'It's a shame we didn't get the chance to see that note up close,' I said instead. 'There might have been something important written on it.'

'Gosh, you're right, Mole. Why didn't I think of that?' At the same time, Armitage removed a scrunched up slip of paper from his pocket and slowly unravelled it.

'That's the note isn't it,' I said, shaking my head at him. 'You stole it.'

'*Borrowed* ... not stole,' insisted Armitage. 'Although I doubt I'll give it back so—'

'That's the same as stealing,' I said. 'I never saw you take it, though.'

'You wouldn't have,' said Armitage smugly. 'Ordinary pimples like you can only see one thing at once. Any more than that and your tiny brains struggle to cope. No, I took it when I pretended to snatch the money back from Madame Isabella. It was a sleight of hand. Neither you nor the unfortunate fortune teller – who we now know not to be blind – had any idea it had even happened.'

Armitage laid the paper flat on the bonnet of the hearse and smoothed out the creases.

'What does it say?' I asked, looking over his shoulder.

'Stop rushing me, Mole,' moaned Armitage. 'I'll tell you when I'm ready. What's that? Oh, I'm ready now. It says ... hide!'

'Hide?' I was about to ask what that could possibly mean when a car sped through the gates of the Cold Crooked Carnival and skidded to a halt beside us. This wasn't any old car, though. This one had flashing lights and a wailing siren.

It also belonged to the police.

Right on cue, a door swung open and a police officer rolled out onto the wet grass.

'This hasn't got anything to do with you, has it, Armitage?' I muttered under my breath. 'Armitage? *Armitage?*'

I turned around, but the private famous detective was nowhere to be seen.

'Where is he?' panted the police officer, breathing heavily as he scrambled to his feet. He was small in size with a squashed face and one long eyebrow that stretched the entire length of his forehead. 'I saw him,' he barked. 'Armitage Hump. So, I'll ask you again. Where is he?'

'I don't know,' I said honestly. 'He *was* here … and then he wasn't. Is he in trouble?'

'Trouble?' The police officer clenched his fists in anger. 'Armitage Hump is a wanted man,' he growled. 'And I won't stop until I've found him!'

8.'SWEETNESS.'

I was about to ask why Armitage was a wanted man when somebody else climbed out of the police car.

It was another police officer, but this one couldn't have been any more different than his angry companion. Dressed in a navy checked suit and shiny shoes, this man was tall and well-built with a thick head of wavy, blond hair, a dimple on his chin and an impressive set of dazzling teeth. Oh, and sunglasses. I glanced up at the sky, even though I already knew it was incredibly dull. The weather in Passing Wind was bad enough, but this was something else entirely. Certainly not the weather for sunglasses.

'Settle down, Constable Smithereens,' said the man softly. 'Rolling about in the grass is no way for an officer of the Crooked Constabulary to behave.'

I struggled not to smile as the two men walked towards me. Stood side by side, they made for the most unlikely pairing I had ever seen. Like chalk and cheese. Or moths and mothballs. Or even myself and Armitage Hump if I'm being honest.

'My name is Inspector Sweetness,' began the man in the

sunglasses. 'There's no need to be afraid; I come in peace. Unlike Constable Smithereens here, I'm the friendly face of the police force. Friendly *and* handsome. I'm everybody's favourite—'

'You're not mine!' cried a voice. It was coming from behind a thick clump of bushes not far from where I was stood.

'Who said that?' asked Sweetness, his head shifting from side to side.

'Nobody,' the voice replied. 'It was just your imagination playing tricks on you.'

'Oh, in that case.' Sweetness turned his attention back to me. 'Where is he? And don't pretend you don't know who I'm talking about. I saw him with my own eyes. I'd recognise old Grumpy anywhere.'

I screwed up my face. 'Grumpy?'

'Grumpy Humpy,' said Sweetness. 'That's just a little name I have for him. Armitage and I are very close. Best friends even—'

'No, we are not!' yelled the voice. 'I'd rather eat my own shoelaces than spend a second in your company!'

Sweetness peered over my shoulder. 'Don't tell me that Grumpy is hiding in those bushes—'

'Yes, don't tell him I'm hiding in the bushes, Mole,' shouted the voice.

'I … um … don't know where he is,' I mumbled awkwardly.

'You might not, little girl, but I most certainly do.' With that, Sweetness marched straight past me. 'Well, well, well, it is you, Grumpy,' he roared, holding out his arms as he edged closer to where the detective was crouched.

'Don't call me that!' Armitage snapped. 'You can call me sir. Or even madam. Or, if you're feeling particularly generous, don't talk to me at all.'

'I thought you two were the best of friends,' I said, confused.

'Worst of enemies more like,' replied Armitage, correcting me.

'We were inseparable when we were younger,' gushed Sweetness. 'We used to do everything together.'

'You used to wrap me up in your mother's nightdress and throw me under the Passing Wind Waterfall,' moaned Armitage. 'You once forced a bucketful of conkers into my mouth and then smashed them with a hammer.'

'Ah, good times,' smiled Sweetness. 'We were just children—'

'*I* was a child,' insisted Armitage. 'You were a swine in short trousers. I didn't sleep for six whole years because of you. I had to go and live in a convent until the nuns threw me out for smuggling goats into my bedroom.'

'You always did have a cracking sense of humour,' chuckled Sweetness. 'Maybe we could carry on this conversation face to face.'

'Not likely,' said Armitage stubbornly. 'I've become quite attached to this bush as it turns out. It's been more of a friend to me than you ever were.'

'Hilarious,' boomed Sweetness. 'Right, have it your way, good buddy, but there's something you must know. I need you.'

'Of course you do,' sighed Armitage. 'What's the matter now? Have you found your first grey hair?'

'Whoa! Nothing that terrifying,' laughed Sweetness. 'I never said it was a national emergency. No, this is strictly police business. I want you to help me stop a robbery, preferably before it happens. You've probably never heard of it, but there's a rotten old chunk of cheese being displayed tomorrow—'

Right on cue, Armitage's head popped up from behind the bush. 'The Stinking Wedge.'

'That's the fellow,' nodded Sweetness. 'Well, the word amongst the rogues and wrong 'uns of Crooked Elbow is that some pretty big nasties from all over the globe are planning on trying to steal this whiffy Wedge of Stinkyness. Turns out, it's quite valuable. Now, I've got twenty-six officers – and Constable Smithereens here, but he only makes up one-third at best – willing to risk their lives to protect it, but I'm not sure that's enough. I was hoping you might join us, Grumpy. You're good at catching criminals. Better than me, at least … and I get paid to do it!'

Armitage began to stroke his chin, deep in thought. 'Just out of interest,' he began, 'how close would you let me get to the Stinking Wedge?'

'As close as you like,' shrugged Sweetness.

Armitage couldn't help but grin. 'Would I be able to … smell it?'

'Of course,' nodded Sweetness.

The grin widened. 'Touch it?'

'I don't see why not,' Sweetness replied.

'Lick it?' asked Armitage, barely able to control his excitement.

'Well ... that's ... erm ... something I might have to think about,' said Sweetness, stumbling over his words.

Armitage, however, was barely listening. 'Take it home and introduce it to Mrs Goose? Knit it a nice jumper so it doesn't get cold in winter? Rub it all over my body like a cheesy shower gel? Stuff it inside my underpants until it begins to melt—?' Armitage stopped suddenly. 'Did I just say all that out loud?'

'Yes, but nobody will think any less of you,' insisted Sweetness. 'So, what do you say, Grumpy? Will you join me at Mysterious Melvin's or not? It's your choice.'

Armitage was already nodding before the Inspector had even finished. 'Of course I—'

'Can't,' I said, butting in. 'Sorry, but it's not possible. You're far too busy.'

'Doing what?' cried Armitage.

'Solving the curse of Crooked Elbow,' I said. 'You haven't forgotten about Constance Snoot already, have you?'

Armitage groaned out loud. 'I had ... until you just reminded me,' he muttered. 'I knew there was a reason I had left Tipsy Towers this morning.'

'Ah, that's a shame,' said Sweetness, shaking his head. 'Still, there's always half a chance the Crooked Constabulary can cope without you. Like I said, I've got twenty-six officers—'

'Twenty-six and a third,' insisted Constable Smithereens, pointing at himself.

'Don't be such a show off,' said Sweetness, wagging a finger at his companion. 'You're only small, remember. I can barely see you if I don't look down. Anyway, I've got twenty-six and a third officers at my disposal. Surely that's enough to … what's wrong now, Grumpy? Why are you crying?'

'No reason,' sobbed Armitage. 'Well, there is one reason. One massive reason. Absolutely enormous. More than anything, I really, really, really want to protect the Stinking Wedge. It would be both an honour and a privilege. Probably the greatest moment of my incredibly miserable life. And yet … as Mole says … I cannot.'

Armitage ducked back down behind the bush. A moment later I heard a series of whimpers followed by a dull *thud*.

Sweetness looked at me, confused. 'What's he doing?'

'I can't be certain,' I began, 'but I think he may be hitting his head on the grass.'

'Is that normal behaviour?' Sweetness asked.

'Not for most people,' I sighed, 'but then Armitage Hump isn't like most people, is he?'

'Certainly not,' agreed Sweetness. 'Maybe I'll just leave him to it. I think I've stirred up enough trouble already, don't you? So long, little girl,' he said, turning away. 'Give Grumpy my love once he finally stops sulking.'

'I'm watching you,' warned Smithereens, jabbing a finger at me as he followed Sweetness into the car. 'You *and* the hide-and-seek champion of Crooked Elbow.'

I assumed he meant Armitage. Talking of which …

'Have they gone yet?' he asked. Crawling out from

behind the bush, Armitage was just in time to see the police car disappear through the gates. 'Oh, thank goodness for that. Sweetness is like a twenty-tier chocolate cake. Too sickly for words.'

'He seemed nice enough,' I said.

'Yes, *too* nice,' frowned Armitage, as he stomped towards the hearse. 'Nobody's that pleasant. Especially when they're at work. That's why I don't trust him.'

'If you say so,' I muttered, opening the passenger door. 'Where are we going now?'

'Drab House,' Armitage replied. 'If we're going to get to the bottom of this curse then it's time to find out a little more about Concrete Snot.'

'You mean Constance Snoot,' I said.

'Yes, her as well,' nodded Armitage, slamming the door shut. 'Right, lets get out of here and never come back.'

'What about Madame Isabella's note?' I asked. 'You never showed it to me.'

A disgruntled Armitage reached into his pocket and grabbed at the slip of paper.

There,' he said, tossing it to me. 'Read it yourself.'

I laid it flat on my lap and smoothed out the creases.

Meet me in the usual place.
7.30 tonight.
Don't be late or you won't get paid.

'We should go there,' I said excitedly.

'Aren't you forgetting something, Mole?' said Armitage.

'We don't know where the *usual place* is.'

'No, but we do know when the Cold Crooked Carnival closes for the day,' I said, pointing at the sign that was hanging from the gates. 'Seven o'clock. We can return when Madame Isabella finishes work and then follow her.'

'So much for never coming back,' grumbled Armitage, as the hearse shuddered into life. 'Sometimes I wish I just kept my mouth shut.'

'You're not the only one,' I said, trying not to laugh as I strapped on my seat belt. 'Oh, sorry. Did I say that out loud?'

Twelve minutes later, Armitage stamped down on the brakes and the hearse skidded to a worryingly sharp halt.

'You can open your eyes now, Mole,' he said. 'We're here.'

Here was right outside a large, stone cottage with a thick, thatched roof and whitewashed walls. 'Are you sure this is Drab House?' I asked.

'Of course I'm sure,' snapped Armitage. 'There's a name sign ... somewhere ... I saw it a moment ago. There's no point you looking for it, though. Everybody knows that moles have particularly poor eyesight ... whoa! Is that what I think it is?'

I followed his gaze and spotted a man in the front garden. Dressed in blue overalls, he was stood at the top of a tall ladder, peering into one of the rooms upstairs.

I had only known Armitage for a matter of hours, but I already knew what he was thinking. 'He might not be a burglar,' I said hastily. 'He could be a … window cleaner.'

'A window cleaner?' Armitage snorted loudly. 'What nonsense! Why would anybody bother to get their windows cleaned?'

'Windows get dirty,' I replied. 'Clean them and they're easier to see through. You should consider that when you get back to Tipsy Towers.'

'Why would I want to see through a window?' cried Armitage. 'There's nothing outside that interests me. Just pimples … and dogs … pimples walking dogs … dogs walking pimples … pimples walking pimples. And birds … I can't stand birds … birds flying … birds singing … birds singing whilst flying—'

'Let's focus on the man in the overalls,' I said, cutting Armitage off mid-flow. 'I still think he's a window cleaner.'

'Except he hasn't got a bucket or a cloth,' Armitage remarked. 'What's he going to clean the windows with? His tongue?'

I didn't like to admit it, but Armitage had a point. That wasn't enough, however, to justify what he did next.

Pushing open the door, Armitage jumped out of the hearse and set off across the garden as fast as he could. The sudden disturbance was enough to make the man in the overalls look down at the ground beneath him.

'Can I help you?' he asked brusquely.

'Yes,' replied Armitage, grabbing hold of the ladder. 'You can help me by holding on to the window ledge.'

The man in the overalls hesitated. 'Why would I possibly need to … don't do that!'

I watched in horror as Armitage pulled the ladder away from the wall. Thankfully, the man had done as he was told. He was holding on.

For how long, however, was anybody's guess.

9.'FALL.'

By the time I had joined Armitage in the garden, the man in the overalls was clinging on for dear life, the pain etched across both his face and his fingertips.

'I'm going to fall,' he squealed. 'I'm going to fall … I'm going to—'

'Fall,' said Armitage, finishing his sentence. 'Yes, I heard you the first time. There's no need to keep on repeating yourself.'

The man in the overalls was still squealing as he switched his attention to me. 'Do something, little girl … I beg you …'

'You're the second person to call me little girl today,' I muttered. Admittedly, now probably wasn't the time to get worked up about it. 'Armitage, please put that ladder back this instant,' I said firmly.

'I'll do no such thing!' cried Armitage, tossing it to one side. 'If I let this sneaky sewer rat climb down now, he'll no doubt scurry off and we'll never see him again.'

'Not true,' whimpered the man in the overalls. 'Why would I run away? I've done nothing wrong. I only wanted to get a cat down. I wasn't going to hurt it.'

'Cat?' I said, confused.

'It's stuck on my roof,' the man in the overalls explained. 'Just outside my bedroom. I saw it stranded up there when I opened the curtains this morning.'

'Your roof? Your bedroom?' I screwed up my face as the truth suddenly dawned on me. 'But then that would make this your—'

'House!' yelled the man in the overalls. 'Of course it is. Why else would I be trying to climb onto the roof?'

I turned to Armitage who, unsurprisingly, refused to meet my eye. 'I should probably fetch that ladder,' he mumbled instead.

'It's too late,' the man in the overalls whined. 'My fingers ... they're slipping—'

'Don't panic,' said Armitage, positioning himself under the window. 'Just let go. I'll catch you. I promise.'

'You won't,' sobbed the man in the overalls.

'I will,' insisted Armitage, holding out his hands. 'You can put your faith in me. After three. One ... two ...'

I had a bad feeling about this. 'Don't do anything silly,' I pleaded.

'What's that, Mole?' I froze as Armitage glanced over his shoulder. 'Did you say something?'

'One,' whispered the man in the overalls. With that, he let go of the ledge ... and landed bottom-first in the flowerbed with a sickening *splat*!

'Don't distract me, Mole,' said Armitage, turning back towards the house. 'Right, where was I? Ah, yes ... one.'

Armitage looked up and then down when he realised there was now a man sprawled out in a heap by his feet. 'Oh, that wasn't supposed to happen.'

'Of course it wasn't.' I waited for the man in the overalls to lift himself out of the dirt before I helped him to his feet. 'Are you okay?' I asked. 'You've had a nasty fall.'

'That was her fault,' said Armitage, jabbing several fingers in my direction. 'She distracted me. It wouldn't surprise me if it was her who took away your ladder as well.'

'No, that was you,' spat the man in the overalls. 'I watched you do it. Are you crazy?'

'Quite possibly,' nodded Armitage, 'but it's never been confirmed.'

'Get away!' cried the man in the overalls, as he tried to hide behind me. 'You're a fiend! A monster! A ... who are you anyway?'

Armitage puffed out his chest. 'I am Armitage Hump, the private famous detective. You've probably heard of me.'

'I most certainly have not,' replied the man in the overalls.

'Oh, there must be something wrong with your hearing as well then,' remarked Armitage, shuffling to one side so he could get a better look inside the man's ears. 'Don't worry; I know just the cure for that. Mole, fetch me as much dynamite as you can lay your hands on and a bicycle pump. That wax won't shift itself—'

'Stop it, Armitage,' I said sternly. 'Can't you see he's distressed enough already?' Sure enough, the man in the overall's legs gave way beneath him and he almost fell over.

'Would you like me to take you into Drab House so you can get comfortable?' I asked.

The man in the overalls stared at me before he spoke. 'Why would I possibly want to go next door?'

'Next door?' My jaw dropped. 'Drab House is next door?'

The man in the overalls gestured behind me. There, partially hidden behind a hanging basket of flowers, was the name sign. 'This is Drub House,' he revealed.

'This is Drub House,' I repeated, reading the sign for myself.

'Yes, of course it is,' mumbled Armitage, shifting awkwardly on the spot. 'I don't know what made you think this was Drab House, Mole.'

I was about to give the detective a piece of my mind when the man in the overalls beat me to it.

'Now do you believe me?' he said, poking Armitage in the chest. 'This is Drub House. It belongs to me. I'm Dudley Drubley.'

'You're what?' frowned Armitage.

'Dudley Drubley,' repeated the man in the overalls.

'No, it's no use,' said Armitage, scratching his head. 'It sounds as if you're gargling water. Let's start again, shall we? What's your name?'

'Dudley Drubley!' the man in the overalls shouted.

'Is that some kind of illness?' wondered Armitage. 'Would you like me to call you a doctor?'

The man in the overalls looked fit to explode. 'My name is Dudley Drubley and I live in Drub House. If you're looking for Drab House it's next door. There's a woman staying there … just don't expect me to say anything nice about her!'

'Really?' Armitage's nostrils twitched wildly. 'Do go on, Double D. I'm all ears.'

'Her name is Constance Snoot,' continued Dudley. 'It was her who put that cat up on my roof. Oh, she said she didn't do it on purpose … she blamed it on her sleepwrecking, whatever that is. I don't believe her, though. No, I'll be pleased when the Drabbles come back from holiday and I never have to see her again.'

'Understandable,' nodded Armitage. 'Do you know her aunt and uncle well?'

'Very well,' insisted Dudley. 'Cynthia and Wilfred Drabble are two of my closest friends. The funny thing is, they don't often go on holiday. Not anything as daring as skiing at least. And certainly not at this time of year. Miss Snoot told me it was a late booking, but I still would have expected the Drabbles to tell me themselves. If you ask me, Snoot's probably got them locked up somewhere.'

'Wow! You don't like Constance Snoot very much, do you?' I said.

'No, I do not,' admitted Dudley. 'I don't like her at all. But then neither would you. Not if she'd stuck a cat on your roof … trampled all over your flowers … thrown eggs at your windows … stuck a banana up your exhaust … used your garden as a lavatory.' Dudley paused for breath. 'You said you were a famous private detective—'

'No, I said I was a private famous detective,' insisted

Armitage. 'Why do you ask?'

'I just wondered what you wanted with Snoot,' said Dudley, perking up a little.

'It's probably best if we don't say,' I replied hastily.

'She's been cursed,' revealed Armitage to my despair. 'We've come to Crooked Elbow to find out who first cast it and then we'll get it removed. That's the plan anyway. I'll most probably get bored and go home early.'

'Curse?' A grinning Dudley picked the ladder up off the grass. 'You don't believe all that magic nonsense, do you?'

'Of course not,' laughed Armitage. 'Although, just to be certain, you're not a witch or a wizard, are you?'

'Well, I for one am extremely pleased you're here,' remarked Dudley, ignoring Armitage's question as he placed the ladder against the wall for a second time. 'The sooner you can get things sorted, the sooner Miss Snoot can leave Crooked Elbow once and for all. Now, would either of you be so kind as to help me get this cat down?'

'There's no need,' said Armitage. 'I watched a cat scamper across your garden moments before I climbed out of the hearse. It must've made its own way down, which also means that there was no need for you to go up there in the first place. Never mind. It's not as if you had a nasty fall or anything, is it?'

Grabbing me by the elbow, Armitage practically dragged me away from Drub House before Dudley Drubley could say another word. It was only once we had swapped driveways and gone next door to Drab House that Armitage finally broke his own silence.

'Double D spells double trouble,' he remarked, far too loudly for my liking. 'I don't trust him as far as I can throw him. And why was he so angry?'

'Because you pulled his ladder away,' I whispered. 'And then laughed at his name.'

'Dudley Drubley,' sniggered Armitage.

'Shush! He'll hear you,' I said, peeking over the garden fence.

'Good,' cried Armitage. 'I want him to hear me. And I also want him to know that he's just flown to the top of my naughty list. From this moment forth, he's my number one suspect. There's a very good chance that it was Double D who cursed Concrete Snot.'

I was hardly convinced, but decided to let it pass. 'Who else is on this naughty list?' I asked instead.

'Well ... there's the unfortunate fortune teller,' began Armitage. 'And ... Mrs Goose—'

'Mrs Goose?' I screwed up my face. 'You think your landlady cursed Constance Snoot?'

'Perhaps,' shrugged Armitage. 'She's the closest thing we've got to a witch ... and then there's ... Sweetness—'

'Inspector Sweetness?' I blurted out. 'I don't think so somehow.'

'He's worse than the Goose,' insisted Armitage. 'And then that just leaves ... you!'

'Me?' I couldn't believe what I was hearing. 'I cursed Constance Snoot?'

'Nice of you to admit it, Mole,' said Armitage, patting me firmly on the head. 'No, seriously. Think about it from my point of view. There I was, fighting with Kevin, and in you walk. A few minutes later and Miss Snot enters too. Now, some pimples might call that a coincidence—'

'Yes, and I'd be one of those pimples … I mean people,' I said.

'But I'd call it highly suspicious,' continued Armitage. 'Maybe you've been planning this whole thing for years. Ever since you were first born. If not before. Maybe you've cursed me as well!'

'You can stop talking now.' We had reached the door to Drab House. Clenching my fist, I knocked three times.

'There's nobody home,' moaned Armitage, almost immediately. 'Snot's not in.'

'You've not given her time to answer,' I argued.

'I've given her at least a second,' Armitage muttered. 'Maybe even two. How much time does she need?'

I was about to reply when Armitage turned his back on me and set off around the side of the house. I followed without thinking and found him leaning against the back door.

'You are going to knock, aren't you?' I said hastily.

'You've already tried that … and look how far it's got us!' With that, Armitage pressed down on the handle and the door opened with an eerie *creak*. 'That was easy,' he grinned.

'We can't just walk in,' I said, pulling the detective back by his jumper. 'That'd be wrong.'

'Yes, it would, wouldn't it.' Shrugging me off, Armitage slipped through the door before I could protest. 'Wrong … but so horribly, horribly right,' he said, chuckling to himself as he invited me inside.

10.'BASEMENT.'

I took a deep breath before I reluctantly joined Armitage in
Drab House.

We were in the kitchen. Despite the unfortunate house
name, the room was brightly decorated and immaculately
clean. Exactly what you'd expect if Constance Snoot's aunt
and uncle were anywhere near as particular as she was.

'What now?' I said quietly.

'Why are you whispering?' shouted Armitage. 'We've
already decided that Concrete Snot is anywhere but here.
We can say and do what we like. Which reminds me. I'm
feeling peckish, Mole. Why don't you open the fridge and
we'll see what's on offer?'

'No way,' I said, shaking my head. 'I'm not stealing Miss
Snoot's food.'

'Oh, I'll just starve then, shall I?' grumbled Armitage.
Without another word, he moved swiftly across the kitchen
and disappeared through the door. I hurried after him and
found that the hallway, much like the kitchen, was neat and
tidy and elegantly furnished.

'Wouldn't you like to live in a house like this?' I asked,

admiring my surroundings.

'What do you think?' Armitage snapped back at me. 'It's got far too many rooms for a start. And far too many rooms means far too much cleaning. And I hate cleaning.'

'I would never have guessed,' I said, trying not to smile. 'You keep Tipsy Towers so spotless.'

'Very funny,' muttered Armitage. 'It'd take me over thirty years to clean that place. I would probably have died of old age before I'd even polished the door knobs … what was that?'

I stopped and looked around. 'What was what?'

'Footsteps,' revealed Armitage. 'They're getting closer … and closer … and … there!'

Armitage rushed over to a door in the middle of the hallway and yanked on the handle. It was locked. Not one to be beaten, he crouched down and peered through the keyhole. 'I can't see much,' he mumbled. 'Only darkness … and more darkness … and … yikes!'

The handle began to rattle, sending Armitage scampering backwards into the wall behind him.

'Is there someone there?' I whispered.

'Someone … or something,' Armitage replied. At the same time he snatched a vase from a side table and clutched it in both hands. 'Get ready,' he warned me. 'Anything could come out from behind that door. A goblin … a dragon … a werewolf … Mrs Goose!'

I frowned at Armitage, who clearly felt the need to explain himself.

'The Goose gets everywhere,' he said. 'I once found her

crawling out of a toilet. I tried to push her back down again, but her legs got stuck in the u-bend.' Armitage leapt behind me as the handle continued to rattle. 'After you, Mole,' he said, pushing me forward. 'Nobody will be overly upset if you get eaten alive …'

I froze with fright as the door finally swung open … and then relaxed a little as Constance Snoot stepped out into the hallway.

'What are you doing here?' bellowed Armitage.

'What am *I* doing here?' A stunned Constance rested on her walking stick for support. 'No, what are *you* doing here?' she shouted back at him.

'Not much really,' admitted Armitage, moving me out of his way. 'We haven't stolen anything if that's what you mean. Mole wanted to, but I wouldn't let her.'

Constance's hands were shaking as she slammed the door shut and locked it behind her. 'Why are you holding that vase?' she asked, glancing over her shoulder. 'You weren't going to hit me with it, were you?'

'Of course not,' said Armitage, lowering his hands. 'I was just admiring it, that's all. It's very … erm … vase-like. May I have it?'

'No, you may not!' replied Constance. Turning sharply, she snatched it from Armitage's grasp and returned it to the table. 'Everything in Drab House has a place … and that place is certainly not back at your dismally dank apartment! Now, how did you get in?'

'The back door,' I said hastily. 'We shouldn't have—'

'Yes, we should've,' argued Armitage. 'We'd been

knocking for ages. You can't expect someone like me to just stand around all day. Mole, however, can be left on any doorstep for any length of time you deem suitable …'

I shot Armitage my steeliest glare, but it didn't appear to faze him in the slightest. 'We are sorry, Miss Snoot,' I said, switching my attention to Constance. 'Whatever our reasons, we shouldn't have entered Drab House without your permission.'

Constance seemed to relax a little as she slipped the key into her pocket. 'Apology accepted,' she said. 'And I'm sorry, too. I'm very jumpy at the moment … you know, because of everything that's happened. I shouldn't have shouted at you. I saw your face, though,' she said, turning towards Armitage. 'It made me panic.'

'It does tend to have that effect on people,' I said.

'Only when those same pimples have got something to hide,' added Armitage. Without warning, he pressed his ear to the door that Constance had only just locked. 'What are you hiding in there?' he asked.

'Hiding?' A clearly flustered Constance shook her head. 'I'm not hiding anything. This door leads to the basement. I would let you down there, but I can't.'

'Can't … or won't?' pressed Armitage.

'Both,' said Constance firmly. 'The basement is flooded. The water pipes must've burst this morning when I was out. Now you can't move in there for water.'

'That's convenient,' snorted Armitage.

'There's nothing convenient about a burst water pipe,' scowled Constance.

'Maybe it's the curse,' I chipped in.

Armitage's response was to elbow me in the ribs. 'Don't give her ideas, Mole. I prefer to watch her squirm under my questioning.'

'Talking of the curse,' began Constance, 'have you been to see Madame Isabella yet?'

'Perhaps,' Armitage replied.

'Yes, we have,' I said honestly.

Constance crossed her arms. 'And?'

'And then we left,' remarked Armitage.

Constance waited for him to speak again. He didn't. 'So, what did Madame Isabella have to say?' she asked eventually.

'Nothing of any interest,' shrugged Armitage. 'I don't think you or your curse made much of an impression on her.'

'That can't be right,' cried Constance. 'You need to talk to her again. When are you planning on going back to the Cold Crooked Carnival?'

'Who said we were?' replied Armitage.

I screwed up my face. 'But I thought—'

Armitage stuck a hand over my mouth before I could finish. 'Ignore her,' he said. 'She does have a tendency to speak without thinking. If I had my way she wouldn't speak at all, of course. Or breathe. Unfortunately, its not for me to … ouch! Don't bite my finger, Mole!'

I didn't. Not really. But I had to do something to get him to remove his hand.

'I'm starting to think that hiring you may have been a mistake, Mr Hump,' said Constance, shaking her head.

'What took you so long to figure that out?' replied Armitage. 'Still, I'm here now so we might as well make the best of it. I hope you've got my room ready, Miss Snot,' he said, heading towards the stairs.

Constance moved quickly to block his path. 'Room?'

'Yes, room,' nodded Armitage. 'Preferably one with a bed in it. A bedroom I think they call it. To cut a short story even shorter, where am I going to sleep?'

'Not in Drab House if that's what you're thinking!' said Constance bluntly. 'I can't just let strangers stay here.'

'Stranger, not strangers,' said Armitage, correcting her. 'There's only one of me. Mole can sleep in the hearse.'

I was about to protest when Constance beat me to it.

'That makes no difference,' she insisted. 'My aunt and uncle wouldn't approve.'

'But then your aunt and uncle aren't here,' argued Armitage. 'They'll never know. I won't leave a mess.'

'You don't have to *leave* a mess – *you* are the mess,' Constance cried. 'So the answer is still no.'

'Ah, that's a shame,' sighed Armitage. 'Maybe you'd prefer it if I forgot about you and your little problem and returned to Tipsy Towers—'

'Wait!' Constance took a breath. 'Let's not do anything rash, Mr Hump,' she said, struggling to smile. 'I do have a guestroom you could use—'

'Perfect.' Without further ado, Armitage set off up the stairs. 'I'll be back soon. I'm just going for an afternoon nap.'

'Stop right there!' I said, pulling Armitage back by his trousers. 'What about me? What am I going to do? There's no way I'm sleeping in that hearse tonight. You can't make me … and if you dare to try I'll go home!'

'Suit yourself,' grinned Armitage. 'If you set off now you should be back before dark.'

I hesitated for a moment before marching into the kitchen and straight out the door. My head was pounding as all manner of thoughts bombarded my brain. What had I done? I couldn't just walk back to Passing Wind, and, besides, it wasn't as if I wanted to. Yes, Armitage Hump was rude. Very rude, in fact. Impossibly rude. And quite horrible at times. But he was also absolutely fascinating. As was the curse of Crooked Elbow.

I stopped when I reached the hearse. What now?

I was still yet to decide when the door to Drab House flew open and out shuffled a clearly disgruntled Armitage. Head down, he was muttering something under his breath as he made his way towards me.

'Sorry,' I said. 'I can't hear you—'

'You can have the guestroom,' he grumbled. 'I'll sleep in the hearse. Just don't rub it in, okay?'

'I won't,' I insisted. 'I promise. And thank you. What made you change your mind?'

'Not what – who,' revealed Armitage, gesturing rudely towards the house. 'Concrete Snot told me it was irresponsible to let a little girl sleep outside by herself—'

'I'm not a little girl,' I said sternly. 'But, yes, she is right. Did Miss Snoot say anything else to convince you?'

'She didn't need to.' Armitage held out his hand. 'Not once she'd given me this.'

It didn't take me long to realise what he was holding. 'Cheese?'

'It sure is,' said Armitage, licking his lips. 'You can have some if you want. It's not as bad as it looks. A little sweaty perhaps, but that's only because I refuse to let it go. Apart from that it's perfect. Smell it if you don't believe me.'

I backed away as Armitage thrust the cheese towards my nostrils. 'I'd rather talk than eat,' I said hastily. 'Have you had any more thoughts about the curse?'

Armitage took a huge bite. 'Just one,' he mumbled with his mouth full. 'Concrete Snot doesn't want us anywhere near that basement. Or her house for that matter. And, for once, it's got nothing to do with my appalling manners … ah, Miss Snot, how nice of you to join us.'

Sure enough, Constance Snoot was coming up the driveway. 'You're still here?' she said, clearly disappointed.

'Naturally,' smiled Armitage. 'I'm not going anywhere. Not until I've had my afternoon nap.'

'I don't pay you to sleep,' snapped Constance. 'I pay you to find out who cursed me. I figured you wouldn't know where to start so I've racked my brains and made a list.'

Constance produced a sheet of folded paper and handed it to Armitage.

'Don't tell me you want us to do your shopping as well?' he grumbled.

'Certainly not,' said Constance. 'No, that's a list of all the people I might have upset recently. You should probably start at the top and work your way down. I'll warn you, though. It is quite long.'

Holding the paper at arm's length, Armitage watched in amazement as it unravelled all the way to his feet. 'Wow!' he gasped. 'There's no *quite* about it. This list is massive! And I thought *I* was disliked.'

'You *are* disliked,' I muttered under my breath.

'Thanks for reminding me,' said Armitage, throwing the list in my direction. 'For a moment there I thought I was losing my touch.'

'Have you two finished?' asked Constance, glaring at us.

'Never,' replied Armitage. 'We'll keep squabbling like this for the rest of the day and beyond. Definitely until we've solved the curse of Crooked Elbow. If I was you I'd go back into Drab House and hang around that basement until it's all over.'

To my surprise, Constance did as he suggested and wandered off without even saying goodbye.

'Well I never,' grinned Armitage, as the two of us climbed into the hearse. 'If I knew it was that easy to get rid of her I'd have tried ages ago. Right, what's the top name on that list, Mole?'

'Ava Hart,' I replied. 'We'll find her at the Heart-to-Hart Dating Agency. She sounds interesting.'

'I'll take your word for it,' frowned Armitage, as he stamped down on the accelerator. 'Hold on tight, Mole. I think it's about time we introduced ourselves to the first of Concrete Snot's many enemies.'

11.'BATTLE.'

I tried not to smile as we pulled up outside The Heart-to-Hart Dating Agency.

Slap-bang in the middle of Cupid Road, the building stood out like a sore thumb amongst perfectly manicured fingers. Every brick, every roof tile, even the chimney pot, had all been painted pink. And not just any old pink either. This was a pink that was so fantastically florescent that even a flamingo would have found it a little overwhelming on the eye. Add to that two heart-shaped windows on either side of a large oval door and what you're left with is something extraordinary to say the very least. Like it or not, The Heart-to-Hart Dating Agency could brighten up any street in Crooked Elbow on even the dullest of days.

And if there was one person who certainly didn't *like it*, it was Armitage.

'I'm not sure I can step foot in there,' he moaned. 'I might catch something. Something highly contagious. The whole place looks so—'

'Pretty?' I said.

'Yes, pretty,' nodded Armitage. 'Pretty revolting.'

I gestured towards the entrance. 'I can always go in first. I don't mind. Just say the word.'

'Word!' Pulling open the door, Armitage shoved me in the back before I could protest. I stumbled forward, but then quickly regained my balance in time to take in my surroundings. Unsurprisingly, the colour scheme inside showed no sign of letting up in the slightest. Everything, from a bountiful chaise-longue sat beside a sturdy triangular desk, to the long luxurious drapes that hung elegantly over a thick, padded carpet, was of the same pink persuasion as the bricks outside.

'This place is like my worst nightmare.' Armitage took a deep breath, pinched his nostrils and followed me into the building. 'The sooner we talk to Miss Fart, the sooner we can get out of here,' he remarked.

'It's Hart,' I said, shaking my head at him. 'You're doing that thing again. When you say everybody's name wrong on purpose because you think it's funny.'

'I'm not doing it to be funny – I'm doing it to be annoying,' insisted Armitage. 'You should know that by now, Mole.'

'Yes, very annoying.' I kept my eyes peeled as I wandered further into the agency. Every inch of the wall beside me was covered with framed photographs. Edging towards them, I soon realised they were close-ups of people's faces.

'I don't mean to be rude …' began Armitage, creeping up behind me.

'Yes, you do,' I said.

'You're right,' Armitage nodded.' I *do* mean to be rude

when I say that they are some of the most unfortunate-looking pimples I have ever set eyes on in my life. To call them ugly would be a compliment. Most of them would've been rejected as extras in a zombie movie, whilst one or two even make Mrs Goose look glamorous.'

'They're not that bad,' I lied. A strange snuffling sound drew my attention away from the photographs. It was Armitage. He was sniffing the air. 'What can you smell?' I asked.

'Powerfully pungent perfume,' he replied. 'The kind that crawls into your throat and scrapes the flesh off your tonsils the moment you breathe! The stink in here is so toxic Miss Fart must be drowning herself in the stuff!'

'You might be able to smell her,' I said, peering around the dating agency, 'but I can't see Miss *Hart* anywhere.'

'No, but Miss Hart can see *you*!'

I jumped out of my skin as a curly mop of fiery-red hair, rosy cheeks and bright crimson lips popped up from behind the counter at the end of the room. It was a woman's head ... and by the grimace on her face she didn't look particularly pleased to see us!

'I know why you're here,' the redhead hissed. 'And it's not because you're looking for love. No, you're looking for trouble. You want to finish what you started, you wicked worm ... you want to silence me forever—'

'Silence you?' Armitage took a moment to think. 'Yes, that would be nice, thank you.'

'He doesn't mean that,' I said hastily.

'Don't I?' shot back Armitage.

'It was you, wasn't it?' A hand joined the head above the counter and pointed an accusing finger at Armitage. 'It's your face that gives you away. If anything, it reminds me of an angry turtle.'

'I've been called worse,' Armitage shrugged. 'And, whilst we're at it, yes, it was me. I mean, in all honesty I have no idea what you're talking about, but you do seem quite irritating so, okay, you win. It … was … me!'

'Well, in that case,' the redhead howled, 'let battle commence!'

I watched in amazement as the head (along with the body that was attached to it) vaulted over the counter, landing not far from where we were stood. Somewhat predictably, the woman was dressed in a smart pink suit and matching stiletto heels.

'Going somewhere nice?' asked Armitage, backing away from her. 'You're far too colourful for a funeral—'

'A funeral?' Crouching down, the redhead removed a single stiletto from her foot. 'Yes, that's a good idea. *Your* funeral!'

Without warning, the stiletto left her hand and flew across the room. I shifted slightly to avoid it, whilst Armitage had to take drastic action and arch his back as the shoe whizzed straight past his nose.

'Charming,' he grumbled. 'Do you greet all your visitors like that?'

'Only the ones I don't like.' The redhead tossed the second stiletto from hand to hand, waiting for the right moment to attack. 'Believe it or not, but I used to be in the circus,' she revealed. 'Knife throwing was my speciality. I could hit an apple from fifty paces.'

'I prefer to eat mine,' said Armitage. 'I swallow them whole. Less messy that way.'

'Messy?' The redhead began to grin. 'Yes, things *are* about to get messy alright. *Very* messy.'

I shuffled backwards until I collided with the wall behind me. Thankfully, the redhead stomped straight past without a second glance. As far as I could tell she only had eyes for a certain detective. Eyes like daggers by the look of things.

'I have to warn you,' said Armitage, raising his fists. 'I'm not afraid to fight back.'

The redhead sliced the air with the stiletto. 'Oh, is that so?'

'No, not really,' Armitage admitted. Unclenching his fists, he held his hands up in defence. 'The truth is I'm afraid to go anywhere near you. Why can't we just talk things over like normal pimples … whoa!'

Hopping to one side, Armitage found himself on top of a delicate-looking glass coffee table as the redhead stabbed the stiletto towards his chest. A moment later the table broke and he was sent sprawling to the ground.

'First you threaten me, and then you break my furniture,' the redhead screeched. 'Well, enough is enough!'

Pulling back her arm, she let fly with the final stiletto. A horrified Armitage hesitated, before rolling out of the way as, like a dart, the shoe embedded itself in the carpet.

'Answer me this,' yelled the redhead. At the same time she searched frantically for another weapon, stumbling upon a long wooden broom. 'Why are you trying to destroy my dating agency?'

'I think you've got the wrong end of the stick,' argued Armitage, as she pushed the broom's bristles towards his face. 'I don't even know you—'

'Yes, you do,' insisted the redhead. 'I'm Ava Hart!'

'*You're* Ava Hart?' I moved away from the wall and tried to position myself between Armitage and his attacker. 'You're just the person we've come to see,' I explained. 'I'm Molly. And that's Armitage Hump. And, yes, as hard as it is to believe, he *is* telling the truth. He doesn't know anything about you or your dating agency. He just wants to ask you a few questions.'

'What? No. Oh, silly me!' An awkward grin spread slowly across Ava Hart's lips as she lowered the broom. 'I thought you'd come here to hurt me.'

'There's always time,' muttered Armitage, climbing wearily to his feet. 'Right, why did you put a curse on Concrete Snot?'

I looked at Ava Hart – or rather the puzzled frown on her face – and decided to fill in the gaps. 'Miss Snoot came to us for help,' I began.

'Came to *me* for help,' insisted Armitage. 'You, Mole, just happened to be in the room at the same time.'

'Somebody has cursed her,' I continued. 'Miss Snoot gave us a long list of suspects and … erm … you were … um—'

'At the very top,' finished Armitage. 'Bad luck, Miss Fart—'

'Hart,' I said, beating Ava to it by a fraction of a second. 'I don't suppose you would know why that would be, do you?'

'Not in the slightest,' replied Ava, shaking her head. 'I've never heard of this Miss Snoot or Snot, and I wouldn't know how to put a curse on somebody even if I wanted to. No, the only person I'm angry with is the rotten swine who keeps on smashing my windows. They've done it every night for the past week. And that's who I thought you were,' added Ava, pointing at Armitage. 'My phantom window smasher.'

'No, but thanks for putting the idea in my head,' mumbled Armitage.

'It's Miss Snoot who's been smashing your windows,' I guessed. 'Not on purpose. The curse has made her sleepwreck in the night.'

'Sleepwreck?' Ava raised an eyebrow. 'Surely you mean sleepwalk.'

'That's what I thought,' I shrugged. 'This is much, much worse, though. Sleepwrecking is sleepwalking with added destruction … what's wrong with you now?'

I stopped and stared at Armitage. Not only was he on his hands and knees, but he also had his eyes closed.

'I can't stay here a moment longer,' he moaned. 'Not with all this pink pickling my brain cells. So, if you've nothing else to tell us, Miss Fart, then I think it's time we bid you a not particularly fond farewell—'

'Hold your horses, Mr Hump,' cried Ava, grabbing Armitage by his belt before he could escape. 'Don't think me forward, but is there anyone special in your life? If not, then this might just be your lucky day. Here at the Heart-to-Hart Dating Agency we don't discriminate against those with more … unfortunate facial failures, so to speak. And you, with your long nose and pointed chin … wrinkled brow and ever-present scowl … yes, you would make quite a catch for a lot of our clients. Especially those who aren't quite so … choosey. To cut to the chase, you're—'

'Out of here,' said Armitage, slipping from her grasp.

'No, I was going to say unique,' Ava called out. 'Many of our clients go for that sort of thing … and I know just the one! Okay, so she's not perfect – far from it, in fact – but if you can see past her flaky skin, rancid breath, crusty nose and scabby lips, then she's actually quite lovely. Better than that, however, she runs her own business.'

'What does she do?' I asked.

'She turns bird poo into chewing gum,' revealed Ava. 'It hasn't quite taken off yet, but there's still time. So, what do you say, Mr Hump? Mr Hump? *Mr Hump?*'

I turned to see the door to the Heart-to-Hart Dating Agency fly open. Through it, the bendy figure of Armitage Hump could be seen galloping away.

'Is that a no?' shouted out Ava.

'Put him down as a maybe,' I said, trying not to smile as I took off after my hot-footed companion. 'He's just shy, that's all. I'm sure I can persuade him.'

12.'WEASEL.'

I was still chuckling to myself as I closed the door to the Heart-to-Hart Dating Agency.

And then I wasn't. In the blink of an eye, the laughter had stuck in my throat and my smile had switched to a frown. There was a good reason for such a quick turnaround, however. And that *reason* was stood right in front of me.

'Miss Coddle, what a pleasant surprise!' remarked Benjamin Bottomley-Belch, my editor at The Passing Print school newspaper. 'Fancy seeing you here.'

'Fancy indeed.' I tried to keep on walking, but Benny seemed reluctant to let me pass. 'What are you doing in Crooked Elbow?' I asked instead.

'What am *I* doing?' Benny glanced over my shoulder at the building I had only just exited. 'Not visiting a dating agency, that's for sure. I didn't think you were that desperate—'

'I'm not,' I said hastily. 'I've been … erm … working.'

Benny snorted. 'Something tells me you've got your priorities wrong, Miss Coddle. The only thing you should be working on is our challenge.'

'Challenge?' I screwed up my face. 'What challenge?'

'Don't tell me you've forgotten already,' said Benny, rolling his eyes at me. 'You promised you could get an interview with Armitage Hump. Or else …'

'Armitage Hump?' I peered over at the hearse. 'Ah, yes, I remember now. There's something I need to tell you—'

'Silence!' said Benny, raising his hand. 'No more excuses.'

'I'm not making excuses,' I shot back.

'A challenge is a challenge,' Benny insisted. 'If you've failed then so be it. And, unless I'm mistaken, you have almost certainly … oh!'

Benny was interrupted mid-sentence by a blaring car horn that refused to stop.

'Sorry,' I mumbled awkwardly. 'He'll give up eventually if you just ignore him.'

Determined to get to the bottom of things, Benny looked around until he finally located the source of the disturbance. 'It's coming from that hearse,' he pointed out. 'There's a man sat behind the wheel … shaking his fist at us. Do you know him?'

I began to nod. 'Unfortunately so. It's—'

'He looks familiar,' said Benny, talking over me. 'I've seen his face before.'

'That would make sense,' I admitted. 'It's—'

'I don't believe it!' Benny blurted out. 'It can't be … surely not … I think it is, you know … it's—'

'Armitage Hump,' I said.

'Armitage Hump,' cried Benny a moment later. 'He's

waving, Miss Coddle. Maybe he recognises me. And now he's … coming over.'

I spun around in horror. It was true. Armitage had given up honking his horn, choosing instead to join us on the pavement.

'Why are we still here?' he grumbled. 'It's not safe. You never know when Miss Fart will pop up and try and take my head off again.' Armitage stopped to give Benny a quick once over. 'Who's this, Mole?' he asked, turning his nose up. 'Your boyfriend?'

'No,' I snapped back at him.

'Certainly not,' spluttered Benny. 'I have standards to uphold. To be the best you have to mix with the best. Talking of which, Mr Hump, what a pleasure it is to meet you.'

'Are you sure about that?' Armitage raised an eyebrow. 'Most pimples run a mile when they see me. They run two miles when I try to kick them.'

'Ah, that's funny,' said Benny, pretending to laugh. 'Do go on, Mr Hump. Tell me more. Oh, where are my manners?' With that, Benny thrust his hand out to be shaken.

'What do you want me to do with that?' frowned Armitage. 'You do realise I've got two of my own, don't you? Mine aren't quite so slimy, though.'

'Yes … erm … still funny.' This time, however, Benny didn't sound quite so convinced. 'My name is Benjamin Bottomley-Belch—'

'I'm sorry to hear that,' remarked Armitage.

'I'm the editor of The Passing Print newspaper,' said Benny.

'And I'm sorry to hear that, too,' Armitage repeated.

'Miss Coddle is one of my … um … writers,' said Benny, flicking a hand in my direction.

'And I'm definitely sorry to hear that!' bellowed Armitage. 'Mole told me she was a writer, but I was starting to have my doubts.'

'Mole?' It took a while, but Benny got there in the end. 'I'll have to remember that,' he smirked at me. 'It suits you.'

I had heard enough. 'Let's go,' I said, grabbing Armitage by the elbow. 'There's somewhere we need to be.'

Armitage, as I'd come to expect after our day together, refused to budge.

'So, you and Miss Coddle know each other,' began Benny, edging closer to the detective. 'I expect she came begging, didn't she? On her hands and knees, promising you the front page? It wouldn't surprise me if she offered you money. Well, I've got a simple message for you, Mr Hump. Ignore her! Miss Coddle … Mole … tries her best, but I'm afraid that's not nearly enough. Not for someone as famous as you. I've had an idea …' Benny ushered Armitage towards him. 'Why don't you give *me* the interview?' he whispered. 'I'm the editor. The top dog. Numero uno. Miss Coddle, meanwhile, is barely even a number. She's a nobody. She doesn't deserve you. Unlike me. So, what do you say?'

'I say that's a wonderful idea,' nodded Armitage.

I screwed up my face. 'Really?'

'Of course not really!' Armitage boomed. He took a deep breath before he spoke again. 'I'm only going to say this once, Mr Bendy Belching Bum, so please listen carefully.'

Benny's bottom lip started to quiver. 'No … that's not my name.'

'I think you'll find it is,' insisted Armitage. 'Let me explain something to you. Mole, as we all know, has many, many faults. She's small … she's not particularly smart … she has a curious stink about her … she talks too much … she even blinks too much. Okay, that's enough. I don't want to bore you with the full list. Yes, Mole has many faults, but there's one thing she most certainly is not. And that thing is a weasel.' Armitage paused. 'You, however, Mr Bendy Belching Bum, are.'

'I … I … I am not a weasel!' stammered Benny.

'You're more weasel than you are human,' remarked Armitage. 'And, like a weasel, you are not to be trusted. Not today. Not tomorrow. Not ever.'

'How dare you!' whined Benny. 'I'll tell my father.'

'You don't need to,' replied Armitage. 'He already knows that you're a weasel. Everybody knows. Even the pimples who don't even know you know. Right, I think I've finished with you now. If I say any more I might hurt your feelings.'

A flustered Benny tried to speak. 'But—'

'I can't hear you,' said Armitage, as he headed back towards the hearse.

'Don't you walk away from me,' cried Benny. 'This is simply unacceptable.'

'I still can't hear you,' Armitage called out. 'Goodbye, weasel. It was … let me think … unpleasurable to meet you.'

'Nice try, Benny,' I said, shaking my head at him. 'Better luck next time.'

And that was how I left the editor of The Passing Print; open-mouthed, stunned into silence, as I hurried to catch up with Armitage.

'I'm very disappointed in your choice of boyfriend, Mole,' he moaned, as I hopped into the hearse. I was about to argue when he pressed a finger to my lips. 'No, don't stick up for him. He's hideous … vile … ruder than me, in fact. Now, I'm not one to interfere, but I don't want to hear the name Bendy Belching Bum ever again. Understand?'

'That suits me,' I said, moving his hand away. 'Shall we talk about the curse of Crooked Elbow instead?'

'Good idea … for once,' said Armitage, as the hearse wheezed into life. 'Look around you, Mole. It's cold, it's dark and it's closing time. Let's head back to the Cold Crooked Carnival and see what the unfortunate fortune teller gets up to after hours. Be warned, though, Mole. Your boyfriend has put me in an even worse mood than usual …'

Thirteen minutes later we reached our destination.

Unlucky for some perhaps, but not us. On fourteen minutes we realised that the time had just passed seven in the evening and the carnival had shut up for the day.

And a few seconds after that we spotted Madame Isabella herself.

Marching out of the gate with her shoulders hunched and her head down, she had switched her frilly dress and bare feet for a long, padded coat and a pair of green wellies. Suitable for winter, of course, but not so much for a mysterious fortune teller.

'Let's get after her,' said Armitage, climbing out of the hearse. 'There's no need to rush though, Mole. How hard can it be to follow a blind woman?'

With that, Madame Isabella grabbed a rickety old bicycle from somewhere behind the gate and began to ride away.

'Very hard,' I sighed. 'Especially when she's not really blind, remember. Now what?'

'Now we shift!' Without another word, Armitage took off after the bicycle. 'I just hope you're as fit as I am,' he shouted back at me.

Armitage was already some distance ahead of me by the time I started to run. Madame Isabella, meanwhile, seemed to have practically disappeared. As far as I could tell she had made it across the large field that I was currently stomping through, swapping grass for concrete in the process.

I pressed on, determined. Yes, I wanted to catch the fortune teller but, more than that, I didn't want to be left behind. Not on my own in the middle of nowhere. Who knows what might be out there?

I had lost sight of Armitage. I could've called out, but opted instead to save my breath and concentrate on where I was heading. Running through grass is never that easy, but running through grass in the dark when you can't see where you're going is practically impossible. Still, at least the field was coming to an end. Bright lights were fast approaching. Soon I would be able to see again.

I was almost there when I took an almighty tumble.

I rolled over several times before coming to a sudden halt. Sitting up quickly, I was surprised to find that the thing that had sent me sprawling was actually curled up in a ball and almost certainly human.

'Is that you, Armitage?' I whispered nervously.

'No, it's the tooth fairy,' grumbled the man himself.

'What are you doing?' I asked, shuffling towards him.

'Sunbathing,' replied Armitage awkwardly. 'What do you think I'm doing, Mole? I'm examining this ...'

I followed his bendy finger and spotted a bicycle. It was the same as the rickety old bicycle that Madame Isabella had been riding.

'She's on foot,' I remarked. 'Which means she'll be slower. We can still catch her, but we have to keep moving.'

'You go,' said Armitage, waving me off. 'I'll meet you there.'

I stayed exactly where I was. 'Are you hurt?'

'Kind of,' mumbled Armitage. 'It's my trousers. They've split.'

I tried not to laugh. 'That's not so bad. Not for somebody like you.'

'Oh, this is worse than it sounds,' muttered Armitage. 'I got them snagged on a prickly bush I ran past. They're ripped to pieces. Practically hanging off me.' Armitage took a breath. 'Just go, Mole,' he insisted. 'This won't be pleasant ...'

I did as he suggested and left him to it. This time I made it all the way to the end of the field without tripping. There I found an open courtyard with a wall that ran all the way around the outside. In the centre of the wall, almost entirely concealed from view, was a passageway. I kept on moving towards it, my senses on red alert. Oddly enough, there was nobody in sight. Not even Madame Isabella. Maybe we had lost her for good.

The passageway was so narrow you could practically touch the wall on either side with your hands in your pockets. The only light was coming from a single street lamp at the opposite end. That was where I spotted the outline of a figure. They were dressed in a long, padded coat and green wellies.

Madame Isabella.

I stepped to one side and hid behind the wall for fear of being spotted. As luck would have it, the fortune teller had her back to me. Now, however, I had a tricky decision to make. I could either stay where I was until Armitage arrived, or I could swallow my fears and confront Madame Isabella myself. I was still considering my options when I took another look.

Now there was another figure under the street lamp. Dressed in a dark cloak, they were barely visible in the shadows.

I already knew because of the note that Armitage had stolen from Madame Isabella that she hadn't stumbled upon the passageway by accident. No, she had gone there for a reason.

To meet someone.

And this was the *someone*.

13.'FRAUD.'

The fortune teller and her mystery companion were deep in conversation.

Their voices were muffled. Madame Isabella was the closest of the two, though, which meant that, if I listened carefully, I could just about make out what she was saying.

'I did as you asked … of course they believed me … Why wouldn't they? … I'm very convincing … besides, I don't think he's as clever as you imagine … okay, I'm not going to argue with you … that just leaves the money … you have got it, haven't you?'

I ducked out of sight a moment later. It was only then that I realised I had been holding my breath. No wonder my heart was pounding so fast.

'I'm coming, Mole!'

I jumped at the sound of my name. Not my *real* name, of course. That would've been far too obvious.

Looking over my shoulder, I saw something speeding towards me.

Something long and bendy on two wheels.

I chose right over left and leapt out of the way as

Armitage rode Madame Isabella's bicycle straight into the wall beside me. Unsurprisingly, both ended up in a crumpled heap. Only one of them was moaning, though. And groaning. And generally making far too much noise for my liking.

'Shush!' I said, pressing a finger to my lips. 'Madame Isabella will hear you.'

'Oh, you've found her,' replied Armitage, scrambling to his feet. 'Hopefully I'll get the chance to tell her how rubbish her bike is. The seat is too low, the tyres are flat and—'

'It's got no brakes,' I said, studying the wall for any sign of damage.

'No, it's *got* brakes,' insisted Armitage. 'I just chose not to use them. I was in a hurry, you see. No time to stop. Talking of which, Mole, shift to one side so I can confront that unfortunate fortune teller and get to the bottom of things. Not *her* bottom, of course. That's far too wrinkly.'

I was about to remind Armitage to keep his voice down when I noticed he was missing something.

'Nice underpants,' I sighed, shaking my head at him. 'Do you think it's acceptable to walk around with no trousers on?'

'Probably not,' admitted Armitage. 'I decided to leave them in that field after they'd split. I'll collect them later. If I'm lucky it'll rain and they'll get washed. First time for everything, I suppose …' Armitage stopped at the opening to the passageway, stretched his neck and took a sneaky peek inside. 'So, where is the old windbag? Ah, there she is. Who's her friend in the over-sized rubbish bag?'

'It's a cloak,' I explained. 'Although I've no idea who's wearing it.'

'We'll know soon enough,' grinned Armitage, rubbing his hands together as he turned back towards me. 'Right, when I say attack, we attack. Things might get ugly so be ready to punch, pinch and poke your way out of there. I'll take the fortune teller and you grab her cloaked companion.'

'That's not fair,' I argued. 'Her cloaked companion could be a dangerous criminal.'

'Okay, have it your way,' muttered Armitage. 'You take her cloaked companion and I'll grab the fortune teller.'

I screwed up my face. 'That's the same thing!'

'Oh, stop complaining,' moaned Armitage. 'Grab who you like. I don't care anymore. Just don't grab me. Right, after three. One … two … whoa!'

A horrified Armitage leapt back in horror as Madame Isabella came charging out of the passageway on two-and-a-half. I was hardly surprised. We had wasted so much time talking she was bound to come out at some point.

Moving swiftly, I tried to catch hold of the fortune teller, but somehow missed completely. Not one to be outdone, Armitage missed as well, although he went one step further and managed, somehow, to do exactly what he warned me not to.

'I've got her!' yelled Armitage, gripping hold of my arm. 'Oh, it's you, Mole. What are you doing between my fingertips?'

In all the confusion, Madame Isabella hauled the bicycle up off the ground and tried to escape. Sure enough, the moment she put foot to pedal, the wheels buckled, the handlebars creaked and the entire bicycle began to shudder uncontrollably. There was only one way this would end … and that *one way* was realised when Madame Isabella hit the ground with a bone-cracking *crunch.*

'We meet again,' said Armitage, resting his foot on the bicycle's frame, pinning the fortune teller beneath it.

'Get off me!' she cried, struggling to sit up. 'I'm innocent … I've done nothing wrong … where are your trousers?'

'Oh, I see your eyes have grown back,' remarked Armitage. 'It's a neat trick, removing your eyeballs whenever you choose.'

I shook my head. 'I don't think that's how it works.'

'Of course it's not,' Madame Isabella snarled. 'I use special patches to cover my eyes whilst I'm at work. It's part of my act. It makes me seem more believable.'

'You're a fraud,' blurted out Armitage. 'You dream up a whole heap of nonsense and then lie to all those pimples.'

A desperate Madame Isabella was squirming about so much that something dropped out of her coat pocket. I picked it up, surprised to find that it was a thick roll of bank notes.

'That's a lot of money,' said Armitage, snatching the notes from out of my grasp.

'That's a lot of *my* money,' hissed Madame Isabella. 'You can't have it.'

'I don't want it,' Armitage shrugged. 'I'll let you have it back in a moment. First, though, you'll have to answer a few questions. Let's start with the money. Where did you get it?'

'A client gave it to me,' replied Madame Isabella.

'Was it your cloaked companion?' pressed Armitage, glancing back along the now empty passageway.

'No.' Madame Isabella spoke too quickly, though. And I wasn't the only one who noticed.

'So it was,' said Armitage smugly. 'Who is he?'

'I never said it was a man,' shot back Madame Isabella.

'Ah, so it was a woman,' said Armitage, raising an eyebrow.

'I didn't say that either,' Madame Isabella argued. 'If I'm being honest, I don't know. They've always covered their face and disguised their voice whenever we've met.'

'And you've never found that strange?' frowned Armitage.

'A bit,' shrugged Madame Isabella. 'But then who am I to complain? Especially when they pay me so much money.'

'To do what?' asked Armitage. 'No, don't tell me. I know already. You were paid to lie to Concrete Snot about the curse of Crooked Elbow. The curse doesn't even exist, does it? You made it up.'

My mouth fell open. I couldn't believe what I was hearing. And, by the look of things, neither could Madame Isabella.

'This is ridiculous,' she mumbled. 'Absurd ... I don't know what you mean ... who's Concrete Snot?'

'Constance Snoot,' I explained.

'Oh.' Madame Isabella seemed to visibly deflate as if all the air had been sucked out of her. 'How did you find out?'

'I didn't,' revealed Armitage, as he finally lifted his foot. 'It was an educated guess ... but you've just confirmed it.'

Pushing the bicycle to one side, Madame Isabella stood up slowly and brushed herself down. 'I didn't want to do it,' she muttered, 'but Nobody insisted.'

'Nobody?' I said, confused.

'That's what they call themselves,' Madame Isabella revealed. 'My cloaked companion. That's all I know so there's no point asking any more questions. Can I go now?'

'Only if you want me to go too,' replied Armitage. 'Go straight to the police! No, you can leave when I say so. And that's not now. Or now. Or now. Or—'

'How did you know which of your clients was Constance Snoot?' I wondered.

'Nobody told me the exact time and date that she would show up,' said Madame Isabella. 'Once Snoot was in my tent all I had to do was break the bad news. She had been cursed. Nobody called it sleepwrecking, whatever that is.'

'It's pretty self-explanatory,' remarked Armitage. 'Doesn't it bother you in the slightest that, since her visit to you, Concrete Snot has made an enemy of nearly every pimple in Crooked Elbow?'

'Yes ... no ... maybe,' said Madame Isabella, stumbling over her words. 'It's not even a real curse so I don't know why she'd still be sleepwrecking. Surely that's something you should be trying to find out, mister detective,' she sneered.

'Oh, I will,' Armitage insisted. 'You might not care about Concrete Snot, but I do.'

'Do you?' I said, surprised.

'No, not really,' admitted Armitage, 'but the unfortunate fortune teller doesn't know that, does she?'

'I can hear you,' said Madame Isabella. 'But not for much longer. I want to go.'

'And I want you to go too,' muttered Armitage, waving her away.

Madame Isabella was about to leave when something caught her eye. 'Can I have my bike back?'

'Be my guest,' said Armitage. 'It's rubbish anyway. The seat is too low, the tyres are flat and—'

'The brakes are good,' insisted Madame Isabella, bending down to pick the bicycle up off the ground.

'I wouldn't know about that,' shrugged Armitage.

I waited for the fortune teller to disappear into the darkness with the battered bicycle by her side before I spoke again.

'Wow!' I gasped. 'So, the curse of Crooked Elbow isn't real. I wasn't expecting that.'

'Why would you?' said Armitage, pulling a face at me. 'I, however, was.'

'And I suppose you know who Nobody is as well,' I said, rolling my eyes at him.

'Maybe,' frowned Armitage. 'Well, I don't, but I will. Sooner rather than later. Then we can get back to Passing Wind.' Armitage spun away from me and set off in the direction of the Cold Crooked Carnival. 'Let's grab my trousers, find the hearse and get back to Drab House,' he said. 'It's getting late. And, besides, I'm starving. I'm sure Concrete Snot will be keen to feed us. Don't look like that, Mole. I'm not asking for a six course meal or anything.' Armitage stopped to think. 'Five will be more than enough,' he decided. 'I'm not greedy.'

14.'GNOME.'

I couldn't sleep.

I don't know why. I was absolutely exhausted and, when the time came to crawl into the bed in the guestroom, my eyes were half-closed and my mind had practically drifted off to somewhere else entirely. It had been a long and bewildering day. Unlike any other I had ever experienced.

And yet, despite all this, I still couldn't sleep.

Constance Snoot had been waiting for us when we had returned from our unusual evening with Madame Isabella. Stood on the doorstep of Drab House, she was carrying a plate of sandwiches, which she promptly insisted we take back to the hearse for fear of getting crumbs on the carpet. After much mumbling and grumbling from Armitage, we eventually did as she requested. We ate in silence, partly because we had nothing to say, but mostly because Armitage had stuffed so much into his mouth he could barely breathe, let alone talk. Once we had finished, I wished him goodnight and returned to the house.

And that was where I found myself now. Laid in bed with my eyes wide open.

The clock chimed midnight.

I rolled onto my back and tried not to shiver. Despite being both fully clothed and wrapped up in a thick blanket, I still hadn't warmed up yet. I already knew I was fighting a losing battle when I started to count sheep. One … two … three …

I heard footsteps on eleven.

Convinced that they were creeping around outside my room, I sat up in bed and waited for Constance Snoot to either knock or just walk in. I had assumed she must have turned in for the night when I had, but maybe I was wrong. Maybe she was going to bed now.

The footsteps stopped and nobody entered.

Resting my head on the pillow, I was all set to close my eyes again when a loud *crashing* sound made me throw back the blanket and jump to my feet. That was nothing like footsteps. Not unless an elephant had charged into the house at some point.

My entire body had gone rigid, but I fought the fear and crept over to the window. Peeking through the curtains, I spotted the hearse parked up outside. If I looked hard enough I could just about make out Armitage's shoes up on the dashboard. He was laid out in the driver's seat, fast asleep presumably. Just where I had left him.

I took a deep breath and tiptoed over to the door. Without overthinking it, I lowered the handle and stepped out onto the landing. There was no sign of Constance, but something else did catch my attention. It was a clock. Or, at least, what remained of a clock. At a guess it had fallen from the wall and smashed when it hit the carpet. I breathed a sigh of relief as I turned back towards the guestroom. There was nothing to worry about, after all. It was just an accident.

Or so I thought.

I was about to close the door behind me when the footsteps returned. This time they were coming from downstairs. Somebody was walking across the hallway.

'Miss Snoot,' I whispered into the darkness. 'Is that you?'

There was no answer so I crept along the landing and took to the top step. I was halfway down the staircase when the front door swung to one side and then slammed shut in quick succession. Whoever had been downstairs had just left Drab House.

Hurrying down the last few steps, I pulled open the door, rushed outside … and crashed straight into a shadowy figure on the doorstep! My first reaction was to dive back inside and slam the door behind me. That failed, however, when the figure stopped it with their foot.

'Ouch!' Armitage lifted his shoe and began to rub it. 'Watch what you're doing, Mole!'

'Oh, it's you.' I took a deep breath as I joined him on the doorstep. 'I didn't realise.'

'I'm not sure I believe that,' frowned Armitage. 'If I had tried to block it with my head you would've slammed it even harder.'

'Probably,' I said, smiling. 'What are you doing here?'

'No, what are *you* doing here?' replied Armitage. 'You should be asleep in *my* room.'

'I heard noises out on the landing and went to

investigate,' I explained. 'I've no idea where Miss Snoot is, though.'

'Oh, I know exactly where Snot is,' remarked Armitage, pointing over his shoulder. Sure enough, Constance Snoot was on the opposite side of the road, kicking the heads off the flowers in every garden she passed. 'She woke me up when she stamped all over the bonnet of my hearse,' Armitage grumbled.

'That doesn't make sense,' I said, shaking my head. 'Why is Miss Snoot still sleepwrecking if the curse of Crooked Elbow isn't even real?'

'Good question,' said Armitage, turning away from me. 'Why don't we ask her? First we have to stop her, though. You trip her up and I'll sit on her.'

I quickly closed the door behind me and set off after Armitage as he, in turn, set off after Constance Snoot. By the time I had caught them both up Constance had already run in front of a car without looking before pushing over several rubbish bins. 'This is dangerous,' I panted. 'What if she has an accident? Or the police turn up?'

'If the police turn up I'll be long gone,' muttered Armitage, peering over his shoulder. 'Knowing my luck, they'll try to arrest me.'

I watched as Armitage spurted forward until he had got in front of Constance. 'Can you hear me, Miss Snot?' he shouted at her. 'Is there anybody home?'

'Don't wake her,' I warned him. 'Not if she's asleep. It's supposed to be bad luck.'

Without breaking stride, Constance barged straight into

Armitage and knocked him clean off his feet.

'No, *that* was bad luck,' he moaned, struggling to stand. 'I knew you should have tripped her up when I told you to.'

Against Armitage's better judgement, we kept our distance as a snoozing Constance continued to wreak havoc through the streets of Crooked Elbow, leaving a trail of destruction everywhere she went. At one point she even passed The Heart-to-Hart Dating Agency, stopping only to push a huge pile of mud through the letterbox, much to Armitage's delight.

'Ha! Miss Fart deserves that,' he chuckled to himself. 'That'll teach her to attack me with her pointy shoe weapons.'

After what felt like several miles of walking, Constance finally came to a halt.

Unfortunately, she came to a halt outside the Crooked Police Station.

'This should be interesting,' grinned Armitage, rubbing his hands together. 'Let's settle in and enjoy the show, Mole.'

The *show* began when Constance picked up a gnome from a garden close by.

'You don't think Miss Snoot is going to throw that, do you?' I said nervously.

With that, Constance pulled back her arm and tossed the gnome high into the sky. Thankfully, it missed the police station and bounced off a nearby tree trunk.

'Yes, I *do* think she's going to throw that,' remarked Armitage a moment later. 'Luckily for her, she's a terrible shot. Otherwise, she'd really be in trouble.'

Right on cue, Constance picked up another gnome and threw it as hard as she could. This time it hit its target.

The police station window.

The glass didn't stand a chance and smashed upon impact. Whether she realised it or not, Constance's response was to hurry away from the scene of the crime as fast as her feet would take her.

'Now *we're* really in trouble,' said Armitage, pulling a face at me. 'I suggest we follow Snot's lead and get out of here quick sharpish.'

'We can't just run off,' I argued.

'Can't we?' said Armitage, spinning away from me.

I watched in amazement as he dived head-first over a wooden fence and disappeared from view. At the same time the door to the police station burst open and out stomped a furious Constable Smithereens.

'You!' he growled, pointing a chunky finger at me.

I looked over my shoulder. 'Who? Me?'

Smithereens lifted his other hand. He was holding the gnome. 'Has *this* got anything to do with you?'

'No,' I said, shaking my head. 'I would never throw a gnome at your window.'

'Who said anything about throwing a gnome at my window?' replied a furious Smithereens.

Whoops. My mistake. 'I'm … erm … innocent,' I mumbled.

'Nonsense,' barked Smithereens. 'There's nothing innocent about a ten-year-old girl stood outside a police station after midnight, especially when a window gets smashed.'

I screwed up my face. 'I'm not ten. I'm—'

'Guilty!' Without warning, Smithereens raced forward and threw himself at me. We hit the ground hard. Not so hard that I couldn't protest my innocence, though.

'I haven't done anything wrong!' I cried.

'That's what they all say,' snorted Smithereens. At the same time he forced my hands behind my back so he could secure them in place with a pair of handcuffs.

'What are you doing?' I said nervously.

'What does it look like?' Taking me by the elbow, Smithereens hauled me to my feet and led me roughly towards the police station. 'Move it, young lady,' he ordered. 'You're under arrest!'

15. 'DAUGHTER.'

I had never been in a prison cell before.

Little more than a store cupboard in size, it had bare brick walls, no windows and a cold, hard floor. The smell that lingered in the air reminded me of rotten cabbage blended with dangerously toxic cleaning products. I was sat on a long metal bench that acted as both a seat during the day and a bed at night. Seeing as it was gone one in the morning, I should really have been fast asleep by now. I wasn't, of course. Instead, I was wide awake with a blanket over my shoulders and my head in my hands.

This shouldn't have been happening. I had done nothing wrong.

Constable Smithereens had thrown me in the cell about half an hour ago and that was the last I had seen of him. He hadn't returned since and I hadn't heard a thing.

Until now ...

The sound of a bolt being pulled across was enough to make me leap up off my seat.

'We meet again.' The door opened with an ear-splittingly loud *creak* to reveal Inspector Sweetness stood in the entrance. Despite the time, he was still impeccably dressed in a sharp suit, bright tie and incredibly shiny shoes. Oh, and sunglasses. Don't forget about the sunglasses. 'It's Mole, isn't it?' he said pleasantly.

'Molly,' I said, correcting him.

'Molly,' nodded Sweetness, as he joined me in the cell. 'Well, this is most unexpected, isn't it? There I was, tucked up in bed, dreaming the sweetest of sweet dreams, when suddenly my phone begins to ring. Who could it be? Well, only Constable Smithereens, that's who. He's blabbering, of course, and extremely angry. I can barely understand him, but two words do stand out above all others. *Armitage Hump.* Almost immediately, I'm up and raring to go. I rush here and … dearie me, there's no sign of old Grumpy anywhere. Just you, little girl.'

'I'm not a little girl,' I said firmly.

'I'm afraid you are,' insisted Sweetness. 'Little … and yet in no way sweet and innocent. Constable Smithereens informs me that you threw a gnome through the police station window. That's atrocious behaviour. Simply unacceptable. Now, seeing as Grumpy is nowhere to be seen, I suggest you tell me your parents' number—'

'No, not my parents,' I blurted out. 'I can't go back to Passing Wind. Not yet. We've got a case to solve first.'

'Ah, yes, the curse of Crooked Elbow,' said Sweetness. 'You mentioned that back at the Cold Crooked Carnival. It's also the reason Grumpy can't help me tomorrow with the Stinking Wedge. So, how are things developing?'

'Investigations are … erm … ongoing,' I mumbled.

'It's going badly then,' chuckled Sweetness. 'So badly that you've wound up in a prison cell in the middle of the night.'

'I didn't do anything,' I cried.

'So, who did?' pressed Sweetness. 'That gnome didn't just fly through the air by itself.' Sweetness paused for thought. 'I mean, it didn't, did it? Because that would be quite spooky.'

'No, it didn't.' I wanted to tell the truth, but knew I couldn't blame it all on Constance Snoot. Not if she had no idea what she was doing. 'It's complicated,' I said eventually. 'But it wasn't me. I promise. I wouldn't ... did you hear that?'

That was a series of curious crashing sounds coming from somewhere else in the police station. Inspector Sweetness must have heard them too because, next thing I knew, he stepped out of the cell so he could look up and down the corridor.

'It's just Constable Smithereens ... I hope,' he muttered unconvincingly. 'He does have a tendency to bang his head against the wall from time to time, especially when he gets frustrated. No, wait one moment ...' Sweetness turned back towards me and forced a smile. 'It seems as if we have a visitor,' he said slowly.

'Where is she? You ... yes, you ... the silly man in the sunglasses ... answer me this instant. Where is she?'

I recognised the voice and then recognised the man himself a moment later as Armitage barged his way into the cell. This wasn't the Armitage I remembered, though. This Armitage seemed to have stolen all of Mrs Goose's clothes, including her hideous brown apron and tatty pink dressing gown, both of which were at least three sizes too small for him. Not only that, but he had stuck a mop head on top of his own hair to give the impression of a straggly grey mess, and coloured in half his teeth with what appeared to be black pen.

'Madam … erm … how nice of you to join us,' remarked Sweetness, scratching his head in confusion.

'Nice nothing,' replied Armitage. 'I'm only here because you've unlawfully imprisoned my daughter.'

I screwed up my face. 'Your daughter?'

'Your daughter?' echoed Sweetness, switching his gaze between me and Armitage in quick succession. 'But that would make you—'

'Her mother,' announced Armitage. 'Yes, that's right. I'm Mrs Coddle. This is my Mole … I mean Molly. She shouldn't be here.'

'Neither should I,' moaned Sweetness. 'I'm supposed to be catching up on my beauty sleep. Yes, that's right. Even someone as fit and fresh as me can't fight back the cruel hands of time.' Sweetness took a moment to run a hand through his silky soft hair. 'Talking of cruel, how did you get past Constable Smithereens?'

'I'm assuming you mean that stumpy little toad who was lurking about in the corridor,' frowned Armitage. 'He's in one of the other cells now. I'm sorry, but he was in my way. And I, Inspector, am not a man to be messed with.'

'A woman,' I said hastily. 'You're not a woman to be messed with … um … Mum.'

'That's right, dear,' nodded Armitage. 'It's an easy mistake to make. Now, where was I? Oh, yes, my daughter. She shouldn't be here.'

'Are you saying she didn't throw the gnome?' asked Sweetness.

'No, not at all,' insisted Armitage. 'Because she did. My Molly smashed the police station window!'

My mouth fell open. 'No … wait … why would you say that?'

'Because it's true, dear.' At the same time Armitage shot me a look. A look that suggested I should keep quiet. 'Let me explain,' he said, turning towards Sweetness. 'My poor daughter suffers from a most unfortunate condition called sleepwrecking. Have you ever heard of it?'

'Regrettably not,' said Sweetness. 'Has it got something to do with wrecking things in your sleep?'

'Oh, what a clever police officer you are!' purred Armitage, placing a hand on Sweetness's wrist. 'You're nowhere near as stupid as I imagined.'

'Thank you … I think,' frowned Sweetness.

Armitage took a moment to wipe an imaginary tear from his eye. 'My Molly has suffered from this unfortunate sleepwrecking for some time now,' he began. 'It's incurable. It also explains why she always has that revolting look on her face. She's just nervous, that's all. Nervous about the damage she might do.' Armitage paused. 'You do believe me, don't you?'

'Sorry,' said Sweetness, distracted. 'I switched off for a moment there. It's not your fault, Mrs Coddle. You're delightful. No, it's the Stinking Wedge. In less than eight hours' time, my good self and the rest of the Crooked Constabulary will be guarding that cherished chunk of cheese with our lives. We need help, though, and there's only one person we can turn to. Are you aware of a lovely, cheery fellow called Armitage Hump?'

'Unfortunately not,' said Armitage hastily. 'He does sound very pleasant, though. And clever. And handsome. And not at all smelly.'

'Your daughter knows him,' continued Sweetness, pointing at me. 'She's currently working on a case with him—'

'She is not working on a case with him!' cried Armitage. 'Armitage Hump works alone. Probably. I mean, I wouldn't actually know that, would I? Because I've never heard of him. Would you like me to shut up now?'

'Never,' said Sweetness, shaking his head. 'I love to hear you talk. But I do have a deal that might interest you, Mrs Coddle. I'm prepared to free your daughter, but there's a condition. I need Armitage Hump. We all do. He's the only one who can protect the Stinking Wedge and keep it safe. Now, if your daughter could just—'

'Yes, I can,' I said hastily. 'I'll talk to him. Armitage will do whatever you want. I'm sure of it. Won't he … um … Mum?'

'I didn't think he had time,' snorted Armitage, pulling a face at me.

'He can *make* time if it means I get out of here,' I said sternly.

'Very well,' nodded Sweetness. 'You can leave, Molly. But I expect to see Grumpy at Mysterious Melvin's Museum of Mind-Bending Marvels first thing in the morning. Would you like me to see you out?'

'There's really no need,' said Armitage, barging past the Inspector. 'Come now, Mole … Molly. Let's get you home before you smash any more windows.'

'Thank you.' I smiled at Sweetness as I wandered out of the cell. 'Ignore my mum. She's pretty strange.'

'Or just pretty,' remarked Sweetness, as he followed me out. 'I don't suppose she's free on Thursday, is she? A spot of dinner perhaps. Who knows where it may lead? Dancing and romancing and—'

'Certainly not,' spat Armitage, turning sharply on the spot. 'I'll have you know I'm a respectable lady. Besides, I like to spend my Thursdays scraping the warts off my face. It's also soup day so they make perfect croutons. Very crunchy.'

'How about the following week then?' pressed Sweetness. 'I won't give up without a fight.'

Armitage was about to raise his fists when I shook my head at him. 'No, I'm still busy,' he said instead. 'Next week is my winter clean. Armpits and ear holes on a Monday. Toes on a Tuesday. Nose on a Wednesday. Both nostrils. Double trouble—'

'In a month then?' begged Sweetness. 'Or two? Three? Six months? A year?'

'Okay,' said Armitage to my surprise. 'I suppose I could go for dinner with you … in a year! It'll probably take me that long to look my best. I'll meet you at the sewage farm at two o'clock in the morning so don't be late.'

'It's a date then,' said Sweetness, blowing Armitage a kiss as we left the police station. 'Until we meet again, fair maiden. Three hundred and sixty-five days and counting …'

Armitage leant into me. 'We need to get out of here,' he whispered. 'Don't run—'

'I'm not,' I insisted. 'You are.'

Sure enough, Armitage had broken into a sprint and taken me with him.

'For one moment there I thought Sweetness might try and kiss me,' he said, refusing to slow. 'I didn't realise I was such an attractive lady.'

'You're not,' I said. 'You're quite grotesque if I'm being honest. Like Mrs Goose's taller, younger, but just as revolting sister.' I paused. 'Sorry. That sounded a bit harsh.'

'I have got feelings, you know,' sulked Armitage. 'Well, I *had* feelings. Once upon a time. When I was a child. Then I got my head stuck in a rabbit hole and things have never been the same since.' Armitage came to a sudden halt beside the hearse. 'I parked here after I returned from Tipsy Towers,' he revealed. 'Mrs Goose wasn't pleased that I took her clothes. I don't think she's got any others so she might be wandering around the house naked until I take them back. Still, at least we're not there to see it. Don't look at me like that, Mole. I was in a rush. I had to get you out of prison.'

'Ah, so you *do* have feelings,' I said trying not to smile.

Armitage made a noise as if he was about to be sick.

'Urrggghhhh! I hope not. Feelings cloud your judgment. They make you slow and lazy. Right, let's get back to Drab House. With any luck, Concrete Snot will have found her own way home. As for me, I need to be in two places at once tomorrow and that's not possible.'

I screwed up my face as I climbed into the hearse. 'Two places?'

'First, I need to find out who dislikes Snot so much that they're willing to pay the unfortunate fortune teller to lie to her,' began Armitage. 'And, second, I need to get to Mysterious Melvin's and protect the Stinking Wedge.'

'You could always snap yourself in half,' I suggested.

'That's one option,' nodded Armitage, as the hearse shuddered into life. 'Kevin the ninja is quite handy with a sword, after all. I'm sure he wouldn't mind slicing me in two.'

'I hope that's a joke,' I said.

'I never joke,' insisted Armitage. 'But I have got a plan. A plan that'll put an end to this curse of Crooked Elbow nonsense once and for all, whilst also making sure that the Stinking Wedge doesn't get stolen.'

I raised an eyebrow. 'What is it?'

'You'll see, Mole,' replied Armitage, tapping his nose. 'You'll see.'

16.'EMPTY.'

I woke late.

Far too late, in fact. I had no idea how much sleep I had managed in the end, but it wasn't much. Only a few hours at best. Not enough for anybody.

Already dressed, I leapt out of bed and hurried downstairs in search of my ridiculously rude companion. I opened the front door, surprised to see that the hearse was no longer there. That was a bad start. If the hearse was missing then Armitage had to be missing too. Unless it had been stolen, of course. But then who would steal a hearse?

'He's not here.' I turned sharply and found Constance Snoot stood right behind me, holding herself up with her walking stick. 'He left early this morning,' she said tersely. 'It was still dark. He woke me by revving his engine.' Constance glanced at her watch. 'You're up late,' she remarked disapprovingly. 'Children are so lazy these days.'

'I had a busy night,' I sighed.

'Busy?' repeated Constance. 'You've only been in bed.'

'Only been in bed?' I could feel myself ready to explode, but somehow held my tongue. 'You don't remember, do you?'

'Remember?' Constance seemed to visibly wobble. 'I've been sleepwrecking again, haven't I?'

I nodded. 'We followed you. You went all over Crooked Elbow. We had trouble keeping up.'

'You should have stopped me,' frowned Constance.

'Armitage wanted to, but I warned him against it,' I had to admit. 'I guess he was right. He can't always be wrong—' A curious repetitive *thud* stopped me mid-sentence. 'What was that?' I asked, looking over Constance's shoulder. 'It's coming from the basement. Maybe we should take a look.'

I was about to do just that when Constance lifted her walking stick and blocked my path. 'One of us will,' she insisted, 'but it won't be you. Like I told you yesterday, there's a problem with the water pipes. Nothing for you to concern yourself with. Oh, maybe it's time you went outside. I think your Mr Hump has finally returned.'

I did as she suggested and found the hearse parked on the driveway. When I looked a little closer I realised there was smoke coming from under the bonnet.

'Is that normal?' I asked, glancing over my shoulder at Constance. Not only had she gone, however, but she had also closed the door. 'Charming,' I muttered to myself. 'Have a nice day, won't you? Maybe we can catch up later.'

'Talking to yourself, Mole, is the first sign of madness,' shouted Armitage, poking his head out of the hearse's window. 'I, naturally, have been doing it for years. But then I don't like pimples, do I? Right, enough about me. What time do you call this anyway?'

'You could've woken me,' I grumbled.

'Yes, I could've,' nodded Armitage. 'But I didn't want to. No offence, but I work better on my own. Nobody under my feet. No silly questions.'

'*I* don't get under your feet and ask silly questions,' I snapped back at him.

'Who said I was talking about you?' replied Armitage. 'I mean, I was. Obviously.' Armitage began to grin, satisfied that he had been his usual rotten self. 'Are you hungry?' he asked, much to my surprise.

'Famished,' I replied honestly.

'Oh, that's unfortunate,' shrugged Armitage. 'You're too late for breakfast and too early for lunch. You're in the hunger danger zone. If you're not careful your stomach will rumble so violently that all your teeth will fall out.'

I chose to ignore both Armitage and the hunger pains that were creeping up on me as I climbed into the hearse. 'It smells funny in here,' I moaned. 'Like sweaty feet. Or mouldy cheese.'

'The dream combination,' said Armitage cheerfully. 'Don't open a window whatever you do. Just savour that fantastically stinky stench.'

I held my nose as Armitage started the engine and the hearse jerked into life. I couldn't stay like that forever, though. Not if I wanted answers to all the questions that were whizzing around my brain.

'Where have you been all morning?' I asked.

Armitage turned to me, confused. 'Me?'

'Of course you,' I said. 'There's nobody else here. And

stop taking your eyes off the road. It's dangerous.'

'I think I drive better when I'm not looking,' remarked Armitage. 'I'm practically perfect when my eyes are closed—'

'Don't you dare!' I said sternly. 'Just concentrate. Please.'

'I thought you wanted to know what I've been up to,' shrugged Armitage. 'I can't concentrate and speak at the same time. It's not possible. You are still listening, aren't you?'

'Not anymore,' I muttered.

Armitage made a strange grunting sound. By the look on his face I must have frustrated him almost as much as he frustrated me. 'Well, I'll tell you anyway,' he said eventually. 'I started out first thing at Mysterious Melvin's Museum of Mind-Bending Marvels. It was still closed, but when have I ever let something as simple as locked doors stop me—'

'You broke in?' I blurted out.

'No, I did not!' argued Armitage. 'I actually got in without breaking anything. Then I spent the next minute or twenty gazing lovingly at the Stinking Wedge. It's amazing, Mole. One of the eight great wonders of the world.'

'It's just a chunk of cheese,' I shrugged.

Armitage slammed on the brakes and the hearse skidded to a halt. 'Get out!' he barked. 'If you're going to speak that way about the Stinking Wedge then there's no place for you in my life. It's not just a chunk of cheese – it's a miracle!'

'Okay, so it's a miraculous chunk of cheese,' I said.

'That'll do,' nodded Armitage. He stepped on the pedal and the hearse grumbled back into life. 'After I'd left Mysterious Melvin's I went to visit some more of those pimples on Snot's Hate List. I saw thirteen in total.'

'Thirteen?' I cried. 'You have been busy. I'm guessing they all told you to go away because you're so rude.'

'Wow!' Armitage stared at me in disbelief. 'That's incredible. How did you know? First, however, each and every one of them informed me that they had never heard of Miss Snot. And you can't hold a grudge against someone you've never even heard of. I should know. I've tried enough times.'

I screwed up my face. 'If none of those people you saw paid Madame Isabella to lie about the curse, then who did?'

'That's what's puzzling me,' admitted Armitage.

I hadn't finished yet. 'And why is Miss Snoot still sleepwrecking if the curse isn't real?'

'Yes, that's puzzling me as well,' Armitage sighed.

I peered out of the window. By the look of things we were heading deeper and deeper into the Crooked Elbow countryside. 'Where are we going?' I asked.

'And that's the third thing that's puzzling me,' confessed Armitage. 'I was hoping you might know.'

'Me?' I frowned. 'But you're driving! You must know where we're going!'

'I did once … just not anymore.' Not for the first time, Armitage stamped on the brakes and the hearse ground to a sudden halt. 'The next name on Snot's Hate List says Brix and Morty's Construction Company,' he revealed, flinging open his door so he could climb out of his seat. 'This is hardly a building site, though.'

Joining Armitage on the roadside, I took a moment to

study the house we had pulled up outside of. 'This is just a crumbling old ruin in the middle of nowhere,' I said accurately. 'And an empty one at that.'

'Empty like the space between your ears,' grinned Armitage. 'Because … you know … you've got no brains. Do I have to explain all my jokes to you?'

'Only the ones that aren't funny,' I replied. 'And that one certainly wasn't … oh, why don't you just walk away when I'm talking?'

Feeling exasperated, I watched as Armitage weaved between huge piles of rubble that led all the way to the house. Without breaking stride, he stomped all over a flattened door in the entrance before disappearing from view. I hurried after him, albeit at a much slower pace for fear of hurting myself. As far as I could tell, my first impression of the house was true. The walls and floorboards were bare and there wasn't a single piece of furniture anywhere to be seen.

Turning to my right, I found Armitage at the foot of a rickety old staircase.

'Brix!' he yelled, his voice echoing around the house. 'Morty! Brix and Morty! Morty and … um … Brix!'

'How many different ways do you want to say their names before you decide there's nobody home?' I said. 'Maybe we should … where are you going now?'

'Upstairs.' Resting his hand on the banister, Armitage took to the first step. 'They must be in here somewhere. They're probably hiding.'

'Why would they be hiding?' I shook my head in despair

as Armitage scampered up the staircase. By the time he had reached the top, large cracks had begun to appear on the steps where he had trodden.

In hindsight, that should probably have been my first warning sign. Unfortunately, I ignored it.

Raising myself up onto my tip-toes, I avoided the cracks the best I could as I set off up the stairs. It was either that or get out of the house entirely and wait in the hearse. Which, thinking about it now, didn't seem like such a bad idea.

The next floor up boasted three bedrooms and a bathroom. Unsurprisingly, a furiously frustrated Armitage had already explored each of them by the time I joined him on the landing.

'It pains me to say it, but maybe you were right,' he muttered begrudgingly. 'This dump is completely empty. Wait until I next see Miss Snot. How dare she send us off on some kind of frantic chicken hunt!'

'Wild goose chase,' I said, correcting him.

'Same difference,' snapped Armitage. 'Do you always have to be so … what's that awful racket?'

I listened carefully, whilst Armitage made his way to one of the bedrooms. Sure enough, I could hear a loud *chugg-chugg-chugging* sound coming from the back of the house.

Armitage returned a moment later, his face split between a smirk and a frown.

'I've got some good news … and some not-so-good news,' he began. 'Just for the record, the not-so-good news is actually bad news. *Very* bad news. Don't let that put you off, though. Right, which one do you want to hear first?'

I swallowed before I spoke. 'Tell me the good news.'

'There's no way you'll be going back to school next week,' Armitage replied.

'Why not?' I asked, confused.

'Because you'll be dead,' said Armitage matter-of-factly. 'That's the not-so-good news. I told you it was bad, didn't I?'

17. 'STUCK.'

It took a moment for Armitage's words to sink in.

'Dead?' I repeated.

'As a doughnut,' nodded Armitage.

'Dead as a doughnut?' I screwed up my face. 'That's not a saying.'

'Well it should be,' said Armitage. 'But just so you know – because I've looked up your nose and I can see that your tiny pea-brain is struggling to take it all in – this house is about to be demolished.' A twisted grin spread suddenly across his lips. 'Goodbye, Mole. It's been nice knowing you ... not!'

Without missing a beat, I ran through to the nearest bedroom so I could take a look for myself. Sure enough, there was an enormous yellow crane sat in the middle of what would've once been the back garden, but was now just a mud bath. Attached to the crane, hanging from a thick chain, was a large steel ball.

Also known as a wrecking ball.

I watched in horror as it moved back and forth, each swing bringing it closer to the house.

'You've got to do something!' I cried, pulling on Armitage's jumper.

'No, I don't,' he said, pushing me away. 'Besides, it's not *me* who's afraid of being squashed. I've had a good life. Well, that's not strictly true. It's been quite miserable actually. And boring. So very, very boring—'

'Please!' I shrieked.

'Don't do that,' moaned Armitage, covering his ears. 'I hate it when you scream. It's bad enough when you just talk. The problem with you, Mole, is that you can't take a joke. Of course I'll do something. There's no need to panic. Not yet, anyway. We've got plenty of time before the moment of impact. At least eighteen seconds … seventeen … sixteen …'

Armitage pressed his forehead against the window for a better view. I followed his gaze and spied a woman inside the crane. As luck would have it she was staring straight into the bedroom. With nothing to lose, I began to shout at the top of my voice whilst waving my hands above my head.

Thirteen … twelve … eleven …

'Is that how you normally behave?' asked Armitage, turning his nose up at me. 'Or should I call an ambulance?'

'I'm trying to get that woman's attention,' I yelled back at him.

Eight … seven … six …

'Leave it to me.' Clambering up onto the ledge, Armitage turned around and wiggled his bum at the window.

It was all to no avail, though. The woman in the crane may have been looking, but she certainly wasn't seeing.

Three … two … one …

The eighteen seconds were up … and the wrecking ball was still swinging!

'Look out below!' Diving backwards, Armitage landed in the middle of the room and rolled over. I followed his lead and threw myself down as the ball made contact.

The damage was instantaneous.

Within seconds, half of the bedroom had crumbled to the ground as the old brickwork fought weakly against the force of the wrecking ball. Luckily for me, the half I was laid on was still intact. Armitage, however, wasn't quite so fortunate. His upper body may have been sprawled across the remaining floorboards, but everything below his waist was dangling over the edge. He was safe … but only just.

'I think my arms are going to drop off!' gulped Armitage, his fingers clawing desperately at the splintered wood. 'Don't just lay there, Mole – help me up!'

I shuffled over and grabbed Armitage by his wrists. Working together, I pulled whilst he wriggled furiously until, with one huge effort, he managed somehow to scramble up onto the remaining floorboards. With Armitage back on solid ground, I took a moment to take in the scene. Where we had once been stood was now nothing but an empty space; that side of the house having been completely demolished.

The wrecking ball, though, was far from finished.

'Scarper!' yelled Armitage, stumbling over his own feet as he tried to make a run for it.

In less time than it takes to agree, I was out of the bedroom and onto the landing. My heart pounding, I refused to slow down as I took to the stairs.

That all changed, however, when I reached the seventh step …

I felt the wood begin to bend as soon as I put my weight on it. Then it split. Before I had a chance to move, my entire foot had been swallowed whole by the crack that had suddenly appeared. A moment later and, as if by magic, the same crack closed around my ankle, trapping me like a vice.

'This is neither the time nor the place to admire the scenery!' bellowed Armitage, crashing into me from behind. 'Keep going, Mole!'

'I can't!' I shouted back at him. 'I'm stuck!'

I had barely finished speaking when the wrecking ball struck for a second time.

The noise was horrendous. I closed my eyes and gripped hold of the banister as the stairs began to violently vibrate. It was only when I opened them again that I realised that the landing, as well as the remainder of the bedroom, had completely vanished. The entire upper floor was now just a thing of the past, leaving the staircase – and Armitage who was stood right behind me – the highest point in the house.

Yes, we had survived. But for how long.

Squeezing past me, Armitage hurried down the last few steps.

'Where are you going?' I cried out, fearing the worst.

'Not far … unfortunately,' Armitage grumbled. 'No, I just need a better angle … and a bit more … swing-ability.'

I was about to ask what *swing-ability* was when Armitage reached into his trouser pocket and removed something long and thin and entirely unexpected.

'You brought your golf club,' I said, shocked.

'Naturally,' nodded Armitage, spinning it around his fingers. 'It goes everywhere with me. It's like an extra limb. Now, try not to panic, Mole. This'll be over before you can say …'

I froze as Armitage lifted the club above his head. A second later I felt a gush of air pass my face, followed swiftly by a loud *crunching* sound. When I looked down, the step had been smashed in two. Better than that, though, my foot was free.

'Move, Mole!' roared Armitage, turning towards the exit.

I didn't need telling twice. Leaping down the rest of the staircase, I trampled all over the door in my haste to flee the building and then kept on running. Armitage should have been slightly ahead of me, but he was nowhere to be seen. I pressed on regardless, desperate to avoid the piles of rubble and debris that were scattered all around. The hearse wasn't far away now. I was edging closer to safety.

'Stop!'

I heard the voice, but chose to ignore it when I realised it wasn't Armitage. What I couldn't ignore, however, was the force of the wrecking ball as it struck for a third and final time. Spinning around to look, I was horrified to see that the rest of the building had collapsed to the ground.

Three swings. That was all it had taken to knock it down.

Three swings and the crumbling old ruin was now nothing but a memory.

'You're trespassing!' shouted a voice. 'This building site is out of bounds!'

My knees buckled as a firm hand dropped down onto my shoulder. Turning slowly, I was surprised to see that it belonged to what appeared to be a werewolf in a black bomber jacket and orange vest. On closer inspection, the werewolf was actually a huge brute of a man with enough hair on both his head and face to fill a fully-stocked wig shop.

'Let go of me!' I moaned, struggling to free myself.

Hairy's response was to press down even harder. 'You're not going anywhere.'

'You're hurting me,' I cried.

'Shame,' laughed Hairy. 'Still, a bit of pain might knock some sense into you—'

'I'll show you the meaning of pain, you fuzzy-faced fiend!'

I heard Armitage before I saw him. When I did see him, however, I could barely believe my eyes. To my amazement, he had emerged from an enormous muddy puddle that had formed on the other side of the road like some kind of human swamp monster. I figured he must have jumped in there moments before the house had finally been destroyed. What I couldn't understand, though, was why.

'Fuzzy-faced fiend?' sneered Hairy. 'Do you think that's funny?'

'Hilarious,' remarked Armitage, shaking himself dry. 'Now, fetch me the organ grinder this instant. It's nothing personal, but I'm sick of talking to the monkey.'

The bristles on Hairy's face began to stand on end. 'Call me a monkey again and I'll lose my temper,' he snarled.

137

'Lose your temper and I'll throw you a banana,' said Armitage. 'In fact, you can have a whole bunch. But first you have to answer one simple question. Where are Brix and Morty?'

Hairy seemed to relax a little as he considered his answer. 'Brix is in that crane,' he revealed. 'She likes to do the demolishing herself.'

'She could've killed us!' I blurted out.

'Not intentionally,' shrugged Hairy. 'It's not her fault she can barely see. Not without her glasses anyway. And I sat on them last Thursday.'

'Brix can't see,' frowned Armitage. 'And yet Morty lets her drive the crane?'

'Yes, I do,' nodded Hairy. 'Because I'm Morty. This is my building site.'

'Why didn't you say that in the first place?' sighed Armitage, rolling his eyes. 'Right, I'm prepared to forgive you and your short-sighted partner, but there's something you need to tell me. What do you know about Concrete Snot?'

'Constance Snoot,' I said, correcting him for the umpteenth time that weekend.

'Snot ... Snoot ... whatever,' mumbled Armitage. 'The fact is she's been cursed. Cursed by you!' he added, pointing at the builder.

Morty took a moment to tug on his beard. 'Cursed by me?'

'Is that you owning up to it?' pressed Armitage.

'No, that's me repeating everything you say,' explained

Morty. 'And I'm only repeating it because I haven't got a clue what you're talking about. Do I look like the sort of person who knows how to cast a curse?'

'Obviously not,' snorted Armitage. 'The only thing I see when I look at you is hair, hair and more hair. It's such a pity. Behind all that furry fuzz I'm sure there's a pretty little face just crying to come out.'

'Right, that's it!' A raging Morty stomped forward, but Armitage simply shuffled to one side to dodge him. Morty tried again, but the same thing happened. 'You're so irritating!' he growled. 'Oh, don't look now, but Brix is right behind you with that crane!'

Armitage turned sharply, but it was all a ruse. There was no one there. No Brix and certainly no crane. At the same time, Morty leapt into action with his fists raised.

'It's a trick, Armitage!' I warned him. 'He's trying to distract you!'

Swivelling on the spot, Armitage grabbed Morty's fist in mid-air before it could collide with his skull. 'What did you say, Mole?' he asked, turning back towards me.

'Ow! That hurts,' whined Morty, dropping to his knees.

'Be quiet, naughty Morty,' frowned Armitage. 'Keep thinking, Mole. If that's possible.'

'I can't remember,' I shrugged. 'Something about a trick—'

'Let go,' pleaded Morty. 'Please … let go.'

'Shush,' snapped Armitage. 'Mole's trying to remember and you keep on distracting her!' With that, he let go of the builder's fist and raced towards me. 'That's it, Mole,' he cried. 'That's what you said. That Morty was trying to distract me.'

I screwed up my face. 'Did I?'

'Indeed you did,' insisted Armitage. 'Now, forget about that hairy lump for one moment and answer this. Why are we here? Think, Mole, think. Why … are … we … here?'

'I don't know,' I mumbled. 'It was you who drove the hearse—'

'No, you wittering wombat,' barked Armitage. 'That's *how* we got here. I want to know *why* we're here?'

'Well … I suppose … the list,' I said. 'Constance told us to—'

'Constance told us to,' repeated Armitage, his eyes widening. 'Of course she did. She gave us the list … the massive list … the impossible list … and sent us on our way.'

Without warning, Armitage turned his back on me and hurried towards the hearse.

'Where are you going?' I called out.

'I'll tell you when we get there, Mole,' he replied awkwardly. 'All you need to know is that I've solved the case.'

'I don't understand,' I said, chasing after him.

'You don't need to,' remarked Armitage. 'Just remember one thing, Mole. The curse of Crooked Elbow is over … but then, if I'm being honest, it never even began!'

18.'STOLEN.'

Armitage drove in silence.

'Where are we going?' That was the fourth time I had asked that particular question. It was also the fourth time that I had been completely ignored. 'Where are we—?'

'I can hear you, Mole,' snapped Armitage. 'I'm just choosing not to answer.'

'Rude,' I muttered.

'Not really,' Armitage replied. 'I'm thinking, that's all. There are lots of pieces to this peculiar puzzle and they all need slotting into place. I'm almost there; it just needs some tweaking. Then we shall be done. The curse of Crooked Elbow will be over and you can start writing that book about me.'

'Oh, yes, the book.' I shifted awkwardly in my seat. 'I don't know how to tell you this … you're not going to like it … but I'm not actually a—'

My stomach leapt up into my throat as Armitage swung the hearse wildly around a sharp bend. I had barely got my breath back when he stepped on the brakes and I lurched forward. I took a moment to recover and then glanced out of the window. We had stopped outside a dismally grey building that was surrounded by police officers.

'Where are we?' I asked.

'Mysterious Melvin's Museum of Mind-Bending Marvels,' replied Armitage.

It took a moment for his words to sink in. 'That's where they're displaying the Stinking Wedge, isn't it?'

'Indeed it is,' grinned Armitage.

'And what's that got to do with the curse of Crooked Elbow?' I moaned.

'Everything,' insisted Armitage, climbing out of the hearse. 'Believe it or not, but I'm not here to drool over that beautiful bulge of champion cheese. That'd be a complete waste of my time. No, I'm just here to check something.'

I was about to ask Armitage what that *something* was when the door to the museum burst open and out rushed Constable Smithereens. Without pausing for breath, he charged towards the hearse, slamming his hands down on its bonnet. 'Gone,' he panted.

'Please tell me you're talking about your boss,' said Armitage, crossing his fingers.

Right on cue, Inspector Sweetness strolled out of the museum. As usual, he was wearing sunglasses. When I looked a little closer, however, I realised he was crying.

'Oh, Grumpy, you're too late,' he sobbed. 'The Stinking Wedge … it's been—'

'Stolen,' said Armitage, finishing his sentence. 'Yes, that would make sense. Ah, never mind. I'm sure you'll get it back at some point.'

'You don't seem very concerned,' I said, suspiciously. 'I thought you loved the Stinking Wedge.'

'I do,' Armitage insisted. 'At this very moment, however, I have more pressing concerns. Don't ask me why, but I need you all to come with me this minute.'

'Even me?' asked Sweetness, wiping his tears away.

'Unfortunately so,' frowned Armitage.

'And me?' asked Smithereens.

'If you must, you curious toad,' Armitage groaned. 'Just try not to get too excitable … hey, don't do that!'

Without warning, Smithereens rolled over the bonnet of the hearse before scrambling through the window of the nearest police car. 'I'll drive,' he shouted at no one in particular. 'Where are we going?'

Armitage wandered over to him and whispered in his ear. Smithereens looked confused for a moment or three before Sweetness joined him in the vehicle and he sped away from the museum.

'What's going on?' I asked, once the hearse was back on the move.

'Nothing,' replied Armitage innocently. 'Well, nothing for you to worry about. The mind of a mere Mole is not strong enough to understand what I'm plotting.'

I screwed up my face. 'Do you have to be so awkward?'

'Do you really need to ask me that?' replied Armitage, without missing a beat.

'No,' I sighed. 'Of course you're awkward. It's one of your greatest skills. Just answer me this, though. Do you know who cursed Constance Snoot?'

'Yes,' nodded Armitage. 'I also know who stole the Stinking Wedge but, for the time being at least, that's not important. First, we have to get to … here!'

I closed my eyes and gripped onto the seat beneath me as the hearse skidded to a screeching halt only inches from the police car. Sweetness and Smithereens were already waiting for us outside. I looked past them and realised where we were.

Drab House.

'Home sweet home,' grinned Armitage. Scrambling out of the hearse, he began to make his way towards the back of the building.

'I thought we were looking for the Stinking Wedge,' said Sweetness, hurrying after him.

'All in due course,' replied Armitage, as he stopped at the back door. 'I won't keep you in suspenders forever … oh, blooming bog goblins! It's locked!'

'Excuse me. What do you think you're doing?'

I switched my attention from Armitage, who was yanking on the door handle with such force that it could easily come off in his hands, to a face that was peeking over the garden fence. It belonged to the next door neighbour.

'What do I think I'm doing?' repeated Armitage snottily. 'That's none of your business, Bubbly Brambly.'

'It's Dudley Drubley actually,' said Dudley, correcting him.

'Is it really?' snorted Armitage. 'Well, in that case, its none of your dudley drubley, Bubbly Brambly. Now, will you please stop staring and go away!'

'How rude!' muttered Dudley, as he ducked out of sight. 'You're undoubtedly the most horrible man I've ever met.'

'Stop flattering me,' said Armitage. 'It's embarrassing.'

'I'll call the police,' mumbled Dudley, as he wandered back towards his own house.

'There's no need,' said Armitage loudly. 'They're already here. Not that you'd know it. Both of them are about as much use as a tennis racquet in a rainstorm.'

'I hope you're not talking about me, Grumpy,' said Sweetness, tapping Armitage on the shoulder. 'Smithereens, yes. But not me.'

'Prove it then,' said Armitage, gesturing towards the door. 'Any idea how we can get through this?'

'Just the one.' Sweetness shuffled out of the way. 'After you, Constable …'

Taking the hint, Smithereens raced straight past us before smashing into the door headfirst.

'Ouch!' I screwed up my face as the wood splintered around the lock and the door flew open. 'That looked painful.'

'That *was* painful,' muttered Smithereens, rubbing his forehead. 'Would anybody mind if I lay down and close my eyes until the throbbing stops …'

'Mind?' echoed Armitage. 'I'd actually prefer it. Right, after you, Mole,' he said, bundling me into the house. 'You never know what might leap out on us …'

I stumbled forward and found myself in the kitchen. 'Miss Snoot … are you here?'

'Of course she's not here!' barked Armitage. 'We've just

knocked her door down. I'd imagine she would've come to see what all the noise was about if she was in.'

Good point. I didn't admit it, though. Instead, I followed Armitage into the hallway. 'What are we searching for?' I wondered.

'Nothing,' replied Armitage, coming to a sudden halt. 'We've already found it.'

I looked around until my eyes rested on the padlocked door beside me. 'The basement?'

Armitage nodded. 'It's been troubling me ever since I first set eyes on it.'

'Are you trying to say that the Stinking Wedge is somewhere behind that door, Grumpy?' asked Sweetness, squeezing between us for a closer look.

'No, I'm not trying to say that at all,' argued Armitage. 'Forget about the Stinking Wedge and concentrate on this padlock. It's thick. Almost as thick as your constable.'

'Talking of Smithereens, would you like me to go and fetch him?' offered Sweetness. 'I'm sure he won't mind using his head again.'

'No, leave this to me.' Positioning himself in front of the basement door, Armitage removed the golf club from his trousers and swung wildly at the padlock. The result was spectacular. Not only did the padlock instantly split in two, but it also dropped to the ground, landing with a horrible *clanging* sound not far from where I was stood.

'Splendid work, Grumpy,' cheered Sweetness, clapping his hands together. 'Sometimes it's best not to use your head if you can help it.'

Armitage pushed open the door to reveal a narrow staircase that led down into darkness. 'I'm not overly fond of basements,' he admitted. 'They always remind me of someone I'd rather not be reminded of.'

'Mrs Goose?' I said.

Armitage shivered. 'Warn me next time you're about to mention that despicable old troll. Now, are you going to stand there all day, Mole, or are you going to lead the way?'

'Me?' I peered down the stairs. 'Why do I always have to go first?'

'You're the smallest,' replied Armitage. 'Which also means you're the least important. That's the way these things work. There's no point complaining about it.'

Reluctantly, I lowered my foot onto the first step.

'Keep your eyes open for anything out of the ordinary,' Armitage said. 'You never know what might be lurking in the shadows.'

'Thanks for your concern,' I muttered to myself. I stopped when I reached the bottom step and felt about for the light switch. One *flick* later and I could see.

The sight that greeted me took my breath away. Armitage was right; there *was* something lurking down in the basement.

'Is that what I think it is?' I whispered in disbelief.

Armitage pushed past me for a closer look. 'Yes, that's exactly what you think it is,' he said. 'It also explains why Concrete Snot didn't want us to come down here.'

'Don't keep me in suspense,' cried Sweetness, eager to join us. 'What is it?'

'It's a pimple,' revealed Armitage. 'And it's alive!'

19.'CON.'

It was actually two pimples … I mean, people.

A man and a woman, they were sat in the corner of the basement, although not through choice by the look of things. Not unless they always decided to sit back-to-back in their pyjamas with their hands tied together and a gag over their mouths.

Rushing over, I knelt down beside them.

'Are you okay?' I asked, once I'd managed to remove the gags. They were both as old as my grandparents with fluffy, white hair and kind, wrinkly faces.

'Of course they're not okay, Mole!' remarked Armitage, coming up behind me. 'They've been trapped in this basement for … let me see … the past fourteen days.'

'Fifteen,' said the man, catching his breath.

'No, fourteen,' insisted Armitage. 'There's no point arguing. It's easy to lose track of time when you're stuck somewhere dark and smelly.' The man was about to speak again when Armitage raised a hand. 'I said don't,' he snapped. 'You were wrong. Get over it. I know I have. Right, why don't you introduce yourselves, Cynthia and Wilfred Drabble.'

'We're ... um ... Cynthia and Wilfred Drabble,' said the woman. 'But then *you* seem to know that already, don't you?'

'Naturally,' nodded Armitage. 'Not only am I thirty-six seconds ahead of everybody else in this basement, I'm also at least thirty-six times smarter.'

'Big head,' I muttered under my breath.

'And you're a small head,' replied Armitage. 'Small head and no brains.'

'Stop it, please,' said Sweetness. 'I hate to hear the two of you squabbling. It makes my bottom lip wobble. Now, is somebody going to tell me what's going on because I haven't got the foggiest. Let's start with the basics. Whose house is this?'

Armitage pointed at the Drabbles. 'Theirs.'

'Ours,' said Cynthia and Wilfred a moment later.

'Your house?' Sweetness slowly shook his head, completely bewildered. 'Call me a jelly-headed joker, but why would you tie yourselves up in your own basement?'

'They wouldn't, you jelly-headed joker!' Armitage blurted out. 'Somebody else did. Somebody else called Concrete Snot.'

'Constance Snoot.' My mouth fell open. 'Surely not.'

'Who's Constance Snoot?' asked Sweetness.

'Their niece,' I replied, nodding towards the Drabbles.

'No, you're wrong,' insisted Cynthia. 'We haven't got a niece. And we don't know anybody called Constance Snoot.'

My mouth fell open again.

'Niece or no niece, what I'd really like to know is what

any of this has got to do with the theft of the Stinking Wedge?' said Sweetness, more confused than ever.

'It's got *everything* to do with the theft of the Stinking Wedge,' replied Armitage sharply. 'That gloriously revolting rock of cheese is the reason I'm here … why we're *all* here … in this basement. It's the reason Concrete Snot … okay, Constance Snoot … walked into my apartment yesterday morning. Except she didn't. Walk in, I mean. Because Constance Snoot doesn't even exist!'

The basement fell silent.

But not for long.

'Oh, very clever, Mr Armitage Hump. I knew you'd figure it out eventually.'

All eyes turned towards the exit. There was someone there, coming down the stairs towards us. It was a woman. A woman that Armitage had only just informed us didn't really exist.

'That's her!' cried Wilfred, pointing wildly at Constance Snoot. 'She's the one who's kept us locked up. Arrest her now, Inspector.'

'Yes, that's a wonderful idea,' nodded Sweetness. 'A splendid idea. A tremendous idea. An idea befitting a police officer of my stature.' Without missing a beat, Sweetness switched his attention to Armitage. 'What do you think, Grumpy?' he whispered. 'Should I arrest her or not?'

'Not … yet,' replied Armitage. 'First, we need to get to the bottom of things. Maybe you'd like to tell us what you're doing here, Constance Snoot … or, should I say, Connie Swindle.'

'Connie Swindle?' Sweetness stopped to think. 'That name rings a bell.'

'So it should, you mumbling meatball,' spat Armitage. 'Connie Swindle is Connie the Con—'

'Connie the Con!' An overjoyed Sweetness began to bounce up and down on the spot. 'Connie the Con is one of the most wanted criminals in Crooked Elbow. She's in the top ten.'

'Number six to be precise,' announced Armitage.

'Fifth actually,' insisted Constance, also known as Connie. 'Soon to be number one. Especially when news breaks that it was me who stole the Stinking Wedge!'

'You!' Sweetness stuck a hand over his mouth in horror. 'You stole the Stinking Wedge? How did you do it?'

'I just wandered in and took it,' said Connie smugly. 'I knew it'd be easy-peasy without Hump there. The Crooked Constabulary aren't really up to much, are they?'

'How rude!' frowned Sweetness. 'I had twenty-six … no, twenty-six *and* a third of my finest officers at Mysterious Melvin's. Still, you've put your foot in it now. Theft is no laughing matter. Just you wait until Constable Smithereens comes and—'

'Is that the same constable that I bumped into outside?' A grinning Connie slapped her walking stick against the palm of her hand. 'He's out cold now, I'm afraid. I didn't hit him hard. I promise.'

'Oh dear,' moaned Sweetness. 'Poor old Smithereens. He really is quite—'

'Useless,' muttered Armitage under his breath.

'A lot like you then, Hump,' remarked Connie. 'I thought you were the best. The finest detective on the planet—'

'Keep going,' said Armitage, urging her on. 'I'm enjoying this.'

'But I was wrong,' continued Connie. 'My plan was simple and yet incredibly effective. I knew the only way I could possibly steal the Stinking Wedge was to keep you away from the scene of the crime. I guessed the police would turn to you for assistance, Hump, and that was why I had to get there first.'

'So you created the tearful Constance Snoot and the ridiculous Curse of Crooked Elbow,' said Armitage, nodding to himself.

'Exactly,' grinned Connie. 'You could hardly be at Mysterious Melvin's if you were busy elsewhere. That list I gave you was completely made up, of course. Yes, I had to go out and cause havoc for a few nights, but that was a small price to pay.' Connie paused. 'What surprised me most, however, is that you fell for it,' she said, shaking her head. 'I barely had to convince you when I came to Tipsy Towers. Your young friend helped, of course. She wanted you to take the case. Forced you to, even.'

'Yes, let's all blame Mole,' agreed Armitage. 'Not just for this, but for everything. The weather ... sloppy dog droppings ... itchy armpits ... the weather again ...'

I ignored Armitage and asked Connie a question of my own. 'You were Nobody, weren't you? You met with Madame Isabella in the passageway?'

'I did more than meet her,' said Connie. 'I paid her to lie about the curse. I wasn't sure it would work, but she was quite convincing. Money talks, after all, and the more I paid her, the better she lied.'

'That's what you think,' snorted Armitage. 'The unfortunate fortune teller told us everything in the end. We knew you couldn't really be sleepwrecking when we followed you last night.'

'And yet you still let me throw a gnome through the police station window,' laughed Connie. 'I thought you were smarter than that, Hump.'

'I am,' insisted Armitage. 'You may think you've pulled the wool over my eyes, but it's me who's been shearing the sheep all along.'

'I don't even know what that means,' Connie shrugged.

'You will do soon,' said Armitage, winking at her. 'Just you mark my words.'

'Right, enough is enough!' said Sweetness sternly. 'If Constable Smithereens is no longer available then I guess I'll just have to come right over and arrest you myself, Miss Swindle.' Sweetness took a step forward … and then two back a moment later. 'Maybe you should come too, Grumpy,' he said, nudging Armitage. 'Strength in numbers and all that. Besides, I think I've hurt my little finger. A splinter perhaps. Or a paper cut. Or—'

'Fine. I'll do it,' muttered Armitage. With that, he set off across the basement. 'Connie the Con, if I was you I'd come quietly …'

'And if I was you I'd stay exactly where I was.' Connie

lifted the walking stick and aimed it at Armitage. 'Take one more step and you'll regret it.'

'Are you sure about that?' said Armitage, trying not to laugh. 'Unless I'm mistaken that's a walking stick you're carrying.'

'Yes, you *are* mistaken,' insisted Connie. Raising the stick to the ceiling, there was a flash of light as a horribly loud *crack* echoed around the basement. I moved quickly and covered my head, whilst Sweetness went one step further and threw himself behind the Drabbles. Only Armitage remained completely still. 'This is no ordinary walking stick,' explained Connie. 'This is a walking stick-cum-gun. Would you like another demonstration?'

'Thanks but no thanks,' said Armitage calmly. 'That is a clever contraption, though. Maybe I can have it. After all, you won't be needing it where you're going.'

'And where do you think I'm going?' smirked Connie.

'Prison, of course,' cried Armitage. 'Do try and keep up. It's not that difficult.'

'Prison?' Connie shook her head. 'Why will I be going to prison? You haven't even caught me. And I've got a gun—'

'A walking stick-cum-gun,' remarked Armitage. 'Get it right.'

'And I've also got the Stinking Wedge,' said Connie, patting her coat pocket. 'I'm leaving now and I don't want anybody to try and follow me.' Connie stopped to think. 'Maybe I should take the girl as a hostage.'

'Girl?' Armitage peered around the basement. 'What girl?'

'I think she means me,' I frowned.

'You, Mole?' Armitage stared at me in disbelief. 'I never knew you were a girl. You're just a child. An awfully annoying, incredibly irritating, particularly pointless child—'

'I don't know what you're trying to do, Hump, but it's not working,' snarled Connie. 'I'm leaving now. No, *we're* leaving,' she said, beckoning me to join her. 'And I think I'll take your car,' she added, turning back to Armitage. 'Give me your keys.'

A disgruntled Armitage stuck a hand into his pocket. 'Are you sure you want to borrow this old heap?' he asked, dangling the keys on the end of his finger. 'It's not really what you'd call a getaway vehicle.'

'I don't care,' snapped Connie. 'And who said anything about *borrowing* it. I'm taking it for good.'

'Suit yourself,' shrugged Armitage, tossing the keys into the air. 'Don't blame me if it breaks down.'

Reaching up, Connie caught the keys one-handed before using her other hand to drag me towards her. 'You can have the girl back when I'm in the clear,' she said, heading up the stairs. 'I'll be long gone by then … never to be seen again—'

'That's what you think!' bellowed Armitage.

I glanced back into the basement and caught sight of a sudden burst of activity. Thrusting his hands deep inside his trousers, Armitage withdrew the golf club in one swift motion and then launched it like a spear. I ducked down, but there was no need to worry. He was aiming for Connie.

And his aim was good.

Connie's reaction, however, was even better.

Spinning smartly on the spot, she used her walking stick to block the club before it harmlessly clattered back down the stairs.

'Oh, that's no way to say goodbye,' Connie grinned. 'This is much better …'

Lifting the walking stick, she pointed it at Armitage's chest … and fired.

I jumped out of my skin as another loud *crack* echoed around the basement. When I looked again Armitage was laying on the floor in a crumpled heap. The bullet had hit him. I was sure of it.

What I wasn't so sure of, though, was if Armitage Hump was dead or alive.

20. 'PLAN B.'

My head was spinning as Connie the Con dragged me out of Drab House and up the driveway.

'Keep moving,' she hissed, but I was barely listening. All I could think about was Armitage. More than anything, I wanted to rush back inside and see if he was okay. Maybe things weren't as bad as they had seemed. Maybe the bullet had only grazed him.

Maybe he was still alive …

'Get in!' A desperate Connie skidded to a halt when we reached the hearse and pulled open the rear doors. I was about to climb inside when she passed me a blindfold. 'Put this on,' she ordered. 'I don't want you to know where we're going.'

I did as she asked and pulled it over my eyes. 'It's too tight,' I moaned.

'That's the least of your worries,' laughed Connie. 'Now, get in and—'

'Miss Snoot … Miss Snoot … have you got a moment?'

It took me a second or two to recognise the voice of Dudley Drubley, the next door neighbour.

'No, I haven't,' replied Connie bluntly. She continued to push, but I stood my ground. Maybe this was my chance. 'Say a word and you'll regret it,' Connie whispered in my ear. I flinched as something poked me in the back. It had to be the walking stick. 'I'm very busy,' Connie called out. '*We're* very busy.'

'This won't take long,' said Dudley. I couldn't see him, but I could tell that he was edging closer. 'It's just … don't think me nosey or anything … but there's been a lot of unusual activity around here this morning.'

'Unusual activity?' repeated a clearly irritated Connie.

'A police car and a hearse for a start,' explained Dudley. 'It all points to … no, I don't suppose that … there's not been a death, has there?'

'Not yet,' muttered Connie under her breath, 'but carry on much longer and …'

'Have your aunt and uncle returned from holiday yet?' pressed Dudley. 'Can I see them?'

'You'll see them soon enough,' remarked Connie. 'Unlike me. I'm leaving now and I'm not planning on coming back.'

'Oh, really,' said Dudley, perking up a little. 'That's such a shame. Still, don't let me stand in your way … why is that girl wearing a blindfold?'

I was about to speak when a loud *crack* beat me to it.

'What was that?' whimpered Dudley. 'It sounded like … a gun.'

'That's because it was,' replied Connie matter-of-factly. 'And if you don't want me to fire again then I suggest you go back to Drub House and keep your nose out of my business!'

With that, Connie grabbed me by the shoulders and bundled me into the back of the hearse. I had barely settled when I heard the driver's door open and then close in quick succession. Laid on my front, my whole body began to violently shake as Connie started the engine and the hearse jerked forward. Before I knew it I was sliding from side to side as we swung around corner after corner after corner after …

'Careful!' I cried out.

'Sorry,' laughed Connie. 'I'm just excited, that's all. I've done it. I've stolen the Stinking Wedge. It'll sell for a fortune. Ha!'

I screwed up my face. I couldn't have cared less about that rotten old cheese, but I did care about Armitage. I hoped with all my heart that he was okay. Because if he wasn't …

Without warning, my entire body rose into the air as the tyres screeched and the hearse came to a complete standstill. Something was wrong. We had only been travelling for a few minutes at most. Certainly not long enough for Connie to think we had escaped from Drab House. I listened carefully, but all I could hear was the groans and grumbles of a hearse that had been well and truly put through its paces.

'Surely not,' muttered Connie to herself. 'It can't be … oh no … it is! It really is! Armitage Hump, you devious devil!' she screamed out loud.

'What's going on?' I asked nervously.

There was no reply. There was, however, a high-pitched *honk* coming from the front of the vehicle. I could only imagine that Connie was pounding her fist – or maybe even her forehead – against the car's horn. And there was only one reason she would do that.

Something – or rather somebody – had made her angry.

'Plan A's been scuppered,' growled Connie, as she started the engine. 'Time for Plan B.'

I rolled over as the wheels spun wildly and the hearse appeared to do a U-turn in the middle of the road. With an ear-piercing howl, we sped off, back (presumably) the way we had just come. Despite the blindfold, I could tell that we were going fast. *Too* fast if anything. It scared me and I didn't like it. And, judging by the way the hearse was spitting and spluttering, I wasn't the only one.

I tried to hold on to whatever I could find, but I was fighting a losing battle. Not only was I rolling about all over the place, but the journey was longer than I had hoped. Wherever we were going, it was out of Crooked Elbow. Finally, we took another sharp bend and the hearse shuddered to a halt. I was still shaking when the back doors swung open and two hands grabbed me by the ankles.

'Get out!' demanded Connie, pulling me from the hearse feet first. I blinked several times as she roughly removed the blindfold. The first thing I could make out was the outline of a tall, lop-sided house directly in front of me.

And the second was a face.

A face so horrifying that I instantly decided I preferred it when I was wearing the blindfold.

'Pleasant surprise, this is.' Stood on the doorstep to Tipsy Towers, Mrs Goose was dressed in the same hideous brown apron over a tatty pink dressing gown that I had seen both her *and* Armitage wearing only yesterday. 'How can me be of assistance?'

Connie turned away in disgust. I knew what she was thinking. That Mrs Goose was one of the ugliest, most vile examples of human *revoltingness* that she had ever set eyes on in her life. No, my mistake. Not *one* of – just *the*. Nobody compared to the Goose.

'The best way you can be of assistance is by not standing so close,' said Connie, waving her away. 'Now let me past. I want to go to Armitage Hump's apartment.'

The hairs that sprouted from Mrs Goose's nostrils began to dance. 'Me don't think Army's home.'

'And?' said Connie.

'And maybe he don't wants you rooting about in there,' remarked Mrs Goose. 'He's a very private man is my Army. He don't like folk interfering with his whatsits.'

Connie hesitated. 'There's a broken window,' she said eventually. 'Armitage asked me to fix it.'

'Blimey, that's a first!' cried a flabbergasted Mrs Goose. 'Army don't usually do nothing me ever asks him. Maybe he's finally falling for me charms.' With that, she gestured along the hallway. 'In you goes,' she said. 'Me won't tell if you don't.'

Grabbing me by the arm, Connie barged Armitage's loathsome landlady out of the way as she marched into the building. Rocking back on her heels, Mrs Goose had other ideas when she saw me, though, and blocked the doorway before I could squeeze past.

'Me likes you,' she whispered, the drool trickling down her chin as she spoke. 'You're very lickable.'

I was about to cry out in horror when Connie reached over and pulled me towards her.

'That old lady's worse than any guard dog,' she muttered. 'At least a dog's got fewer fleas.'

'Why are we here?' I asked.

'You'll see.' Connie stopped at Armitage's apartment and pulled on the handle. The door swung to one side, but Connie didn't move. I couldn't be sure, but something seemed to have spooked her. Edging closer, I peeked over her shoulder to see what had stopped her so suddenly. The sight that greeted me was unexpected to say the least.

'Surprise,' laughed a tall, bendy man in the middle of the room. 'What took you so long?'

21.'SWAP.'

The sight of Armitage Hump stood in his own apartment was almost enough to make me cry out with joy.

Almost … but not quite.

The fact that Connie the Con was there as well did put something of a dampener on things. And let's not forget about the walking stick. That was hardly ideal either.

Not that Armitage seemed to mind. Smiling brightly, he ushered Connie into the room as if the two of them were long lost friends re-united for the first time in years.

'What are you doing here?' she scowled, refusing to move from the doorway. 'You're supposed to be dead.'

'Am I really?' Armitage threw up his hands, theatrically. 'That's the problem with me. I'm always such a huge disappointment.'

'I shot you,' said Connie.

'No, you shot *at* me,' said Armitage, correcting her. 'The bullet, however, missed me by a cat's whisker. Or is it a bee's beard? Or a goat's goatee? Regardless, you fired, I fell over and the rest, as they say, is history.'

With small, shuffling steps, Connie made her way

cautiously into the room with me right beside her. She kept her walking stick raised and her eyes on Armitage at all times. Before I knew it, we were stood on the exact same spot as Armitage when he had taken his shower under the drips from the Darling's apartment the previous day.

'What have you done with it, Hump?' Connie asked.

'Done with what?' shrugged Armitage.

'You know what I'm talking about,' Connie growled. 'The Stinking Wedge. Somebody managed to switch it at Mysterious Melvin's before I got a chance to steal it. They replaced it with half a brick. They were almost identical except for one major difference. A brick doesn't stink!'

A grinning Armitage patted his trouser pocket. 'Unlike this …'

'So, it *was* you who switched it,' said Connie, her eyes widening. 'I thought you might hide it here at Tipsy Towers. I never imagined you would just hide it about yourself, though.'

'Always expect the unexpected,' replied Armitage smugly. 'Despite what I told Sweetness, I always feared that some naughty pimple might try and steal this sublime slab of cheese whilst it was on display. That's why I took a trip to Mysterious Melvin's first thing this morning and nabbed it myself! I figured that not even the most ferocious of Wedge lovers would study it too closely … largely because no one really knows what it looks like! Admittedly, I wasn't entirely convinced that you were the thief at that point, although I did have my suspicions. You looked so familiar, you see. I never forget a criminal's face and a quick rummage through my miraculous memory confirmed it. Constance Snoot was Connie the Con. What a turn-up! I also knew that when you fled with Mole, it wouldn't take you long to see through my brick replacement and come looking for the real thing.'

'Great story, Hump,' groaned Connie, rolling her eyes. 'Really interesting. Now, stop wasting time and give me the Stinking Wedge. Then you can have the girl.'

'What sort of deal is that?' moaned Armitage. 'I love the Stinking Wedge. I barely even *like* Mole.'

'Armitage!' I yelled.

Connie pressed the walking stick against my head. 'I'm not joking, Hump!'

'Neither am I,' insisted Armitage. 'Mole's been nothing but trouble ever since she first turned up here. If it wasn't for her I'd have spent an enjoyable few days throwing my old underpants at Mrs Goose. But, oh no, Mole had to come along and ruin things!'

Connie pushed the walking stick so hard that I cried out in pain. 'Give me the real Stinking Wedge!' she hissed. 'Or else!'

Armitage opened his mouth … and yawned. I wondered if he was as brave as he was making out or just incredibly tired. Either way, the effect was as if someone had waved a red rag at a raging con artist.

'I'll do it,' spat Connie, her finger twitching on the trigger. 'I've already shown that I'm not afraid to shoot.'

'Shoot … and miss,' grinned Armitage. As an afterthought, he held out his hand. There, sat proudly in his palm, was a small, brown lump of something indescribable.

I guessed it was the real Stinking Wedge.

'Okay, Connie, you've got yourself a deal,' said Armitage, much to my relief. 'I agree to your swap. The Wedge for the Mole. In hindsight, I've decided I don't despise her with every inch of my being, after all. She's … erm … almost … um … tolerable … in her own way.'

'You say the nicest things,' I muttered.

Stepping forward, Armitage held out his hand … and then pulled it away at the last moment. 'One last thing,' he said, irritatingly. 'Before we swap, let me offer you a simple piece of advice.'

'Advice?' Connie gritted her teeth. 'You can take your advice and stick it!'

'Yes, but stick it where exactly?' said Armitage. 'Now, if I had my way I'd stick it in your ears, because this is something you really need to hear.'

'I mean it, Hump,' cried Connie, waving the walking stick wildly around the apartment. 'I'm not interested.'

'No, but you should be,' remarked Armitage. 'Just listen and learn. It's only two words. Very simple to understand, even for someone as cloth-eared as you. Right, here we go … look up.'

The apartment fell silent.

'Don't play games with me,' spat Connie, staring straight ahead.

'I'm not,' insisted Armitage. 'Look up.'

Whether she wanted to or not, Connie's stubbornness was preventing her from lifting her eyes and doing as Armitage suggested.

I, however, had no such trouble.

It was only then that I realised what Armitage was talking about. Directly above us, the ceiling was sagging like an enormous water balloon ready to burst. The drops that fell regularly were now bigger and much more frequent then they had been when Armitage had taken his shower. Less a drip and more of a dribble, a puddle had even formed on the floorboards beside me. I couldn't understand why I hadn't spotted it earlier, but then neither had Connie.

That was her second mistake.

Her first was to think she could get one over on Armitage Hump.

'This is your last chance,' warned Connie, shaking with anger. 'Give … me … the … Stinking … Wedge!'

Armitage gazed lovingly at the lump of cheese in his hand and began to speak. 'Everyday, for as long as I can remember, Morning and Evelyn Darling have played … I can't quite bring myself to say this, but here goes … *music* that could make even the toughest ears bleed. Then they dance. Badly. The effect is like a herd of stampeding mud wrestlers stomping all over my forehead. The problem for you is that they tend to play this … *music* at two particular times of the day. One is ten o'clock in the morning. Also known as shower time. And the other is three o'clock in the afternoon. Also known as not shower time. Now, I don't think I need to tell you, Connie, that three o'clock is fast approaching. Trust me, the moment that … *music* starts something very bad will happen to you. So, why don't you do yourself a favour and look up. Then we can do something about it.'

Connie didn't say a word. Instead, she lifted the walking stick, aiming it at Armitage's nose. 'You've had your fun; now it's my turn,' she snarled. 'I'm going to enjoy this—'

'Not as much as I am!' blurted out Armitage. 'Swap!'

As the grandfather clock in the corner of the room struck three, Armitage tossed the Stinking Wedge high into the air. Right on cue, the first notes of music could be heard in the apartment above. A moment later and the volume was cranked up to full blast.

Springing into action, Connie let go of both me and the walking stick so she could catch the cheese before it hit the ground.

'I did try to warn you,' yelled Armitage, lunging forward. I felt my feet leave the ground as he pulled me towards him. I had barely landed when an almighty *crash* filled my ears. It was followed by a high-pitched yelp from Connie. She had caught the Stinking Wedge, before finally deciding to look up. That was the exact moment the ceiling collapsed and the entire bathroom suite from the apartment above came tumbling down into Armitage's room. Try as she might, Connie was powerless to prevent the sink from landing right on top of her.

As well as the bath.

And, most revoltingly of all, the toilet.

'What's going on in here?' Mrs Goose's eyes popped out of their sockets as she poked her head through the door. 'That lady,' she wailed. 'The posh 'un ... she's been well and truly flattened!'

'Make yourself useful, Goose, and ring the police,'

ordered Armitage. Spinning his landlady round by her shoulders, he shoved her out of the door before she could say another word. 'Ask for Inspector Sweetness. Tell him that Connie Swindle is in my apartment. She's going nowhere. She's—'

'Using the facilities,' I chipped in.

'Precisely,' grinned Armitage, crouching down so he could retrieve the Stinking Wedge from its resting place amongst the rubble. 'Connie the Con is otherwise occupied.'

It didn't take long for the police to clear up the mess.

Inspector Sweetness – sunglasses and all – was in and out of Tipsy Towers before I had even got my breath back. Whilst Connie was being handcuffed and dragged away by the ever-eager Constable Smithereens, other members of the Crooked Constabulary searched for evidence amongst the contents of the Darling's bathroom suite. As luck would have it they took everything away, leaving Armitage's apartment in much the same state that it had been in before. Granted, there was now a gigantic hole in the ceiling, but then Armitage had never been that house proud to begin with.

Sweetness was almost out the door when he came to a sudden halt. 'May I have it please?'

A distracted Armitage tried to ignore him for as long as possible, before reluctantly handing over the Stinking Wedge. 'Gosh! It really does reek!' moaned Sweetness, placing the cheese in a large metallic briefcase, which he then strapped to his wrist. 'Now, don't think me an overeager beaver, Grumpy, but if you ever fancy helping me out with any of my cases, I'd be more than willing to welcome you with open arms.'

'Well, I won't think you overeager, if you don't think me rude,' Armitage replied.

'Rude?' repeated Sweetness. 'You haven't been rude.'

'Not yet I haven't,' grinned Armitage. 'But it's coming. Right about ... now. Quite simply, Sweetness, you great dollop of donkey dung, I'd rather wipe my nose on a badger's behind than spend another hour in your company.'

'Fair enough,' said Sweetness cheerfully. 'It's your choice, I suppose. Still, just to be certain, is that a definite *no*, an uncertain *maybe*, or even a possible *yes?*'

Armitage stuck out his tongue and blew a raspberry until Sweetness finally got the hint and left us to it. 'Mysterious Melvin's reward will be in the post,' he called out from the hallway. 'Spend it wisely. I know a lovely little boutique on the outskirts of Passing Wind if you're interested. They do a lovely range in sunglasses. Very stylish.'

'Goodbye, Sweetness,' said Armitage, slamming the door shut. 'See you soon ... just not too soon ... preferably not at all.'

'You could fix your apartment with that reward money,' I said, glancing up at the hole above me. 'Starting with that not so tiny crack in your ceiling.'

'I used to like that crack in the ceiling,' sighed Armitage. 'It kept me company at night. Good friends like that are hard to come by.' Armitage took a breath. 'You'd better be off, Mole,' he said, gesturing towards the door. 'We wouldn't want your parents to think you were never coming home. It'd only get their hopes up.'

'Funny.' I made my way to the door but stopped before I got there. 'There's something I need to tell you,' I mumbled awkwardly. 'I … um … lied. Sorry, but it was the only way I could get into your apartment. The thing is—'

'You're not really writing a book about me,' finished Armitage. 'I know that already, Mole. Doesn't mean you can't, though. Not if you want to. You can do anything you like. And no big-headed bossy boots like Bendy Belching-Bum can tell you otherwise.'

I smiled. He was right, of course. I could write a book if I wanted to. And I did. I *really* wanted to. More than anything.

'The problem with that, however,' began Armitage, refusing to meet my eye, 'is that you'll have to keep on returning to Tipsy Towers. I mean, I'm not overly keen, but you could always come back … tomorrow.'

'Tomorrow?' I repeated.

'Well, don't then!' sulked Armitage. 'See if I care. I've got plenty of things to be getting on with. I don't need you rabbiting on in my earhole all day long—'

'I never said I wouldn't come,' I insisted. 'But I'm at school tomorrow. Next weekend would be good, though. If you're sure.'

'Not really,' shrugged Armitage. 'You are quite irritating, after all. And small. But, yes, I suppose I'm prepared to see through your faults, Molly.'

'Molly?' I screwed up my face. 'You never call me Molly.

I can't believe I'm about to say this,' I said, trying not to laugh, 'but I think I prefer Mole.'

'I thought you would,' nodded Armitage. 'Now, be off with you and I'll see you next Saturday. Not too early, of course. Everybody needs their beauty sleep. You more than most.'

Opening the door, I was all set to leave when my eyes were drawn to the other side of the room. There was something climbing through the window.

No, not something.

Someone.

Someone I had seen before.

Someone dressed entirely in white.

'Yesterday you were lucky,' panted Kevin the ninja, trying to catch his breath as he balanced on the window ledge. 'Today ... maybe not so.'

My heart skipped a beat as he leapt into the air with not one, but three swords. One in each hand and a third clenched tightly between his teeth.

'Not you again.' Without missing a beat, Armitage stepped forward and removed the golf club from his trouser pocket, ready for the duel ahead. 'After you, Kevin,' he said, grinning from ear to ear. 'I'm ready when you are ...'

22.'QUIT.'

The next day I wandered into the newsroom (also known as the school canteen) and placed a single piece of paper right under the nose of Benjamin Bottomley-Belch.

'Oh, hello, Miss Coddle.' The editor of The Passing Print newspaper glanced up at me, surprised. 'I wasn't expecting to see you.'

'Why not?' I said, taking a seat at the table. 'I'm still a part of this newspaper, aren't I?'

'For now,' smirked Benny. 'Been busy, have we?'

'Extremely,' I said. 'But then you would know that, wouldn't you? Because you saw me.' I paused for effect. 'You saw me with Armitage Hump.'

Benny squirmed as all eyes turned towards him. 'Well, yes, that's true,' he mumbled. 'But it's not an occasion I recall with any fondness. He's rude, isn't he? Your Mr Hump?'

'Amongst other things,' I sighed. 'He's not an easy person to get on with. The time I spent with him was very interesting, though. Not to mention incredibly scary—'

Benny interrupted me with a yawn. 'You're boring us

now, Miss Coddle. Why don't you get straight to the point. Have you got a story for me or not?'

I gestured towards the paper I had placed on the table.

Benny turned it over and shrugged. 'There's nothing on it.'

'Well spotted,' I replied. 'No wonder you're the editor.'

'You haven't written a word,' cried Benny. 'But that means … yes … you've lost!'

I waited a moment before I spoke again. 'Are you sure about that?'

'Of course I'm sure!' roared Benny. 'Only you could spend a weekend with Armitage Hump and fail to write a single word. You do remember our little challenge, don't you?'

'Vaguely,' I said. 'Perhaps you'd like to remind me.'

'It'll be my pleasure,' said Benny, shaking with excitement. 'If you had managed to get a story I would've given you the front page. But you didn't. You failed. And that means one thing and one thing only—'

'I'll see myself out,' I said, standing up.

Benny's mouth fell open. 'No, you don't just get to leave – I have to fire you first!'

'Benjamin has to fire you first,' repeated Ursula word for word.

'There's no need,' I said, heading towards the door. 'I quit!'

'You can't,' spluttered Benny. 'Nobody quits The Passing Print. Not unless I say so.'

'Not unless Benjamin says so,' echoed Ursula.

'Be quiet, Miss Fawn!' Benny yelled. 'This is neither the time nor the place for you to do your impression of a human parrot. As for you, Miss Coddle, I've got a job that—'

'I'm not doing it,' I said, pulling open the door. 'In fact, I'm leaving.'

'Don't you dare!' spat Benny. 'If you walk out now there's no coming back.'

'Yes, that's the idea,' I said, setting off along the corridor. 'So long, everybody. It's been … frustrating.'

'Wait!' pleaded Benny. 'What are you going to do now?'

'Write a book,' I shouted back at him. With every step, the distance between myself and The Passing Print school newspaper grew wider. 'It's called The Curse of Crooked Elbow,' I added under my breath. 'You can read it when I've finished.'

THE END

ARMITAGE HUMP WILL RETURN

IN…

THE BEAST OF
BACK O'BEYOND

OTHER BOOKS BY THE AUTHOR

THE GREATEST SPY WHO NEVER WAS
(HUGO DARE BOOK 1)

Meet Hugo Dare. Schoolboy turned super spy. Both stupidly dangerous and dangerously stupid.

A robbery at the Bottle Bank. Diamond smuggling at the Pearly Gates Cemetery. The theft of priceless artefact, Coocamba's Idol. Hugo is there on each and every occasion. but then so, too, is someone else.

Wrinkles, the town of Crooked Elbow's oldest criminal mastermind.

In a battle of good versus evil, young versus old, ugly versus even uglier, there can only be one winner … and it better be Hugo otherwise we're all in trouble!

THE WEASEL HAS LANDED
(HUGO DARE BOOK 2)

Schoolboy turned super spy Hugo Dare is back … and this time he's going where others fear to tread!

No, not barefoot through a puddle of cat sick. This is much, much worse than that.

Maya, the Mayor of Crooked Elbow's daughter, is being held captive in one of the most dangerous places known to mankind.

Elbow's End.

Populated by rogues and wrong 'uns of the lowest order, only one person can find Maya and get her out of there in one piece. Unfortunately, that person is busy flossing their nostrils so it's left to someone else.

And that someone else is Hugo!

THE DAY OF THE RASCAL
(HUGO DARE BOOK 3)

Teenage super spy Hugo Dare returns. That's the good news. The bad news is he's faced with his perilous mission yet. We'll come to that in a moment …

The Day of the Rascal. A day when the whole of Crooked Elbow falls foul to the devilish antics of one devious little delinquent. The year, however, the Rascal has turned the screw. No more childish pranks and elaborate stunts for him. No, this year he plans to take out the Chief of SICK … and I don't mean for dinner! He wants to finish him off. Eliminate, eradicate and exterminate. RIP the Big Cheese.

Hugo is soon on the case. His instructions are simple. Stop the Rascal before it's too late. Easy-peasy. With any luck he might even be home in time for breakfast.

If only that was true …

THE HUNT FOR HUGO DARE
(HUGO DARE BOOK 4)

Schoolboy-turned-super spy Hugo Dare is used to danger. He lives it every day. Morning noon and night. Some might even say it's his middle name. (That's ridiculous. Who would ever say that?) This time, however, things are even more dangerous than ever.

Pursued at every turn by a wretched pack of undesirables, Hugo more use all his skills to shake them off and, ultimately, stay alive. It's anything but easy though, and with the streets of Crooked Elbow no longer safe, where can he go when everywhere spells trouble (not literally)? Who can he trust when he can't even trust himself (that's probably not true either)? And will he ever get the chance to ditch his school uniform for something a little more sophisticated (I'm guessing he will)?

The Hunt for Hugo Dare has begun ... and only one young spy can make sure it doesn't end in disaster!

ACKNOWLEDGEMENTS

Thanks to the wonderful Sian Phillips for her eagle-eyed editing skills and glowing praise.

Thanks to the wonderful Stuart Bache and all the team at Books Covered for the front cover.

Thanks to everyone at the wonderful Polgarus Studio for their first-rate formatting.

Note to self – look for another word other than wonderful. Do not forget. Because that would be really embarrassing. I'm embarrassed enough already just thinking about it.

AUTHOR FACTFILE

NAME: David Codd. But you can call me David Codd. Because that's my name. Obviously.

DATE OF BIRTH: Sometime in the past. It's all a little hazy. I'm not entirely convinced I was even there if I'm being honest.

BIRTHPLACE: In a hospital. In Lincoln. In Lincolnshire. In England.

ADDRESS: No, thank you. I don't like the feel of the wind against my bare legs.

HEIGHT: Taller than a squirrel but much shorter than a lamppost. Just somewhere in between.

WEIGHT: What for?

OCCUPATION: Writing this. It doesn't just happen by accident. Or does it?

LIKES: Norwich City football club, running, desert boots, parsnips.

DISLIKES: Norwich City football club, running, rain, Brussels sprouts.

REASON FOR WRITING: My fingers needed some exercise. They were getting lazy, just hanging there, doing nothing.

ANYTHING ELSE: Thank you for reading this book. If you've got this far then you deserve a medal. Just don't ask me for one. Because I haven't got any. But I am very grateful. And do feel free to leave a review on Amazon if leaving reviews on Amazon is your kind of thing. It's not easy for a new author so please be kind.

Until the next time …

Printed in Great Britain
by Amazon

28973024R10108